# EAST BROTHER

ATOPON BOOKS

Atopon Books
907 15th Street
Santa Monica, California 90403
United States



First edition by Urizen Books, 2020



Publisher's Cataloging-in-Publication data
Names: Mattessich, Stefan, author.
Title: East Brother / Stefan Mattessich.
Description: Santa Monica, CA: Atopon Books, 2023.
Identifiers: LCCN 2022946080 | ISBN: 978-0-578-57261-1 (paperback) |
Subjects: LCSH Friendship--Fiction. | California--Fiction. | Counterculture in literature. | Gentrification in literature. | Drug Addiction.
BISAC FICTION / General | FICTION / Contemporary | FICTION / Magic Realism
Classification: LCC PS3613.A4353 E32 2023 | DDC 813.6--dc23

Cover Image: "Cedar Point Amusement Park" by Jeff Warneck on 123RF@COM

Printed in the United States of America.

Man is a metaphorical animal.
—Nietzsche

1

# On Liberty

Seaman Jess Cooper stood looking backward from the fantail of his ship, a guided-missile destroyer barreling through dead of night and a sleety mist that shot past like an army of routed ghosts. The roar of the screw churning water beneath him might almost have been their lamentations. He thought to report that but decided against it, calling in for about the twelfth time, "All conditions normal." He blew his air horn, alerting the void to his whereabouts.

He was at the tail end of a low visibility midwatch, cold and stiff in the neck, with nothing but a thermos of black coffee for comfort. Darren, supposed to relieve him, was late.

It'd been a long day, or a long ten days underway off the California coast, going through various simulations, replenishments at sea, shore bombardments, walkdowns. The ordeal promised to end in the morning, when they pulled in to port at North Island.

He heard Darren cross the flight deck behind him. When the ship pitched too sharply, he stumbled to the tarmac.

"Fuck!"

Jess went to meet him. Darren started on hearing the scuff of his shoes. He blurted out, "Who's there?!"

Jess rolled his eyes. "I'm the one who should be asking that, Darren."

"Right," he said, rubbing the elbow he'd landed on. "Sorry."

"Did you check in?"

"Yeah. Go on. Get out of here."

He went to his quarters and climbed into his rack, the top one. Bone tired, he'd only just conked out when a bell rang and someone yelled, "Fire! Fire! Class Charlie Fire in the main machinery room!"

He groaned with his seven bunkmates. Another drill. He peeled himself from the overhead and made for the door in total darkness, everybody jostling everybody else. It was like that all through the passageway and up the ladderwell. By the time he was above deck, the power came on and he was told to go back down.

The ship had reached San Diego Bay in the meantime, and by reveille it was pierside. His final duty, after an hour spent chipping perfectly good paint from steel with a needle gun, consisted of passing knuckleboxes in a line above deck to be offloaded. That done, he was on liberty till morning. He'd arranged to hang out with his friend Chris, then stationed on a berthing barge till his ship got out of drydock. They met in their civvies at the Del Taco in Coronado.

Chris took Jess straight off to see this guy he knew in San Diego, a Rastafarian living out of his van, who sold them two hits of acid. Neither seaman knew what they were in for as they dissolved the tabs on their tongues. But they were intent on getting away from the Navy for a while—the farther the better.

They wandered around the downtown, the waterfront, in this big hotel going up and down the escalators, and for a while everything seemed under control. They spent what felt like hours on a broad concrete plaza set high above the bay, raptly absorbed in the spectacle of arriving container ships, commercial jets flying low over the city, ribbons of cars on freeways and bridges. San Diego looked immense and miniature at the same time, its intricately moving parts synchronized with all the pleasing precision of a complicated watch. But after a while that indivisible quality in the scene turned static, intensifying into toy-like irrelevance, and it became the uneasy emblem of a more enigmatic isolation, a huge fragment, as disconnected from anything real as a city built on a fairy's wing.

They managed to get on a bus headed to the beach before the drug shifted into its ultra-paradoxical phase and they no longer knew where they were going, or why. They didn't know which way was up or down, backward or forward, near or faraway. To Jess, walking on the shoreline, it seemed as if someone had taken his thumb and smudged out the horizon. The setting sun was unchained from the earth and from Venus when it squeezed into the sky at dusk. The torn solar system drifted apart in his mind. Was he hurtling downwards, or spinning out in a wide centrifugal arc? He felt himself moving through stray currents, through magnetic fields of celestial origin as they swept across the surface of the earth. His body shimmered, lost in its own contours, a fluid without dimension, flowing as the universe always flows he supposed, only it wasn't a unity but a dispersion, a-cosmic and disintegrating like a vast prismatic fractal.

All night long they went from one bar to another. People were filmy images on a bubble that kept floating away. Jess couldn't take them seriously. Even good-looking girls couldn't make him desire them. It was hard to talk because he had no grip on the person talking, his motivations, his voice, the airy sentience of his breath. He'd entered this no-man's land of himself where nothing willful made any sense. He had to grab Chris by the shoulder every now and then just to prove that he was really there.

How he returned to base on time he would never be able to reconstruct. He was plagued by a feeling of déjà vu. It wouldn't go away no matter what effort of concentration he made. This left him so distracted that he showed up for quarters in his dress blues. His commanding officer said, "Seaman, it's May and three hundred thousand men and women are wearing their whites."

"Yes, sir," stuttered out Jess.

"Why aren't you?"

"I forgot, sir."

The commanding officer didn't like the tone of his voice. He got up close in his face, boxed the side of his head with his palm, and said, "What kind of a haircut is that?"

Jess answered as best he could: "I don't know what kind of haircut, sir."

This pissed off the commanding officer even more, and he had a couple of MPs escort him to the brig. He found himself in a jail cell with another man whose face was pitted and scarred by acne. He was a real Popeye, with eyes set wide apart like a fish, no chin, and a huge round nose. Jess noted four stripped off hash marks on his sleeve; he was still a seaman's apprentice after all those years. He'd probably been demoted so many times he didn't care what he was anymore. He sat slumped over on the opposite bunk and didn't say a word when Jess came in. He just stared. Pretty soon he lit a cigarette, but after the first puff he perched it on his knee and forgot about it. His eyes fluttered closed and he fell asleep right where he sat. The cigarette slowly burned. Jess watched the ash grow longer and longer, till it started to stain his skintight pant leg. He kept thinking, "I'm in the brig, man, this is the brig I'm in." But somehow he couldn't keep the significance of this fact securely in his mind. He also wasn't about to wake the guy up. It was all he could do to convince himself that the man, the cigarette, the brig, all of it hadn't happened before, a thousand times before, over and over again like the kid who kept crying wolf.

Two more MPs came and took him to be interrogated by a captain. Jess answered his questions, but he couldn't hide the fact that he was disoriented. He kept glancing off at nothing, convinced that someone else was there, this invisible person who watched him from some different but parallel world. The captain asked if he'd taken anything while on R&R. Jess had sense enough to deny it. "No, sir," he said, "I never, ever take drugs harder than alcohol, sir. I swear to God."

The captain could tell he was lying. But rather than give him the drug test, he said, "Well, if you aren't stoned, then you must be crazy, seaman." He turned to the MPs. "Put this man in the observation ward at Camp Pendleton. We'll let the psychiatrists deal with him."

He knew Jess wasn't crazy. He did it just for spite, to teach him a lesson. And the lesson was he had to spend eight days in the loony bin with a bunch of Marines who really were crazy. First thing that happened was this doctor, who looked as mean and square-jawed as his sergeant in boot camp, mustered all the inmates and introduced Jess to the ward. He glared at him with more malevolence than he had ever seen in another person.

"You're not a headcase, seaman," he said. "I can tell a headcase when I see one, and I can tell a lazy-ass sonofabitch who thinks he's gone on a holiday, too." He wiggled his way in close to Jess (why do the officers all do that?), so close his hips and shoulders were touching his and he could see chunks of lead filling the cavities in his teeth when he opened his mouth.

"Do you hear me, seaman?" he screamed. "You're not loco. You're a malingerer! Understand? A malingerer!"

He shuffled back an inch or so, just enough to get this beak-like pointed finger in Jess's face so he could jab it at him on the second syllable of that last word. "A malingerer!" he cried. "A malingerer! A malingerer!" The finger got so close the nail even nicked his chin and drew blood, but all Jess could do was stand at attention and take it, the deep hallucinogenic spell he was under clearing at last into a cold fear of the actual.

That's when he started to ask himself, as he never had before, what he was doing there—not only in the ward but in the Navy, in San Diego, by the ocean, next to a desert, close to Mexico. Why this, rather than some other place altogether? Why this life, rather than some other like the one he felt in the intense hold the drug had on him? He never thought too much about why he joined the military. It seemed to be the smartest move, all things considered. After high school he didn't have any direction. He sat around trying to think up something to do, but nothing occurred to him. This blankness seemed like it would never go away, like it was just the natural outgrowth of a personality not too sure of itself in the first place. He'd always been too vague, too touched by solitude. His parents worried about that. They made him play soccer and little league baseball because they thought team sports would wipe away the sensitive streak in his nature. He liked playing games, but he never took to them either. Always when the time came to give that extra effort, to gut it out past the pleasures of being on the field, smelling the grass, feeling the warm sun on his face, he lost interest, a palpable dread took over.

The same thing happened at school, and it really kicked in after he graduated. Because no one around him saw it as anything except a problem, he himself never understood, maybe he still didn't right up to those days in the ward, that fundamentally his life bored him. He found it hard to want the things he was supposed to want, whether that meant grades, girls, popularity, whatever. There was an element of sketchiness in others and in himself that robbed him of incentive. He didn't feel this way because he thought he was missing out on an exciting alternative busy happening somewhere else. Maybe it was happening somewhere else, but he didn't consider his chances of getting there all that good, and even if they were he didn't imagine it would be enough to make him care. He had enough humility, or he lacked enough self-respect, to see that his life wasn't the story of some fiery passion doused by the cold waters of other mediocre people. That would be too dramatic and already out of the ordinary, and he was just ordinary. A normal, mediocre kid. He had no fire in him. That's what the coaches and teachers and career counselors said, and he had no particular reason to think they were wrong. He'd been lit by a flame that would not burn. This idea followed him wherever he went, because it wasn't any different from him. That's how he put it when he mulled the problem over in his head: he couldn't burn himself up, he couldn't rid himself of himself.

All he liked to do, and could do without losing interest in the end, was draw and listen to music. He had a knack for art, and he learned some guitar, too, but none of it led anywhere. He realized in his pre-Navy doldrums that these things were fun because they confirmed him in his dread rather than helped him to change it. He could listen to music for hours, laying alone on his bed with the shutters closed and the lights dimmed, but where did that get him? He could draw faces of the people he saw at the Home Depot where he worked, but how was that more than daydreaming? He sensed that solitude had consequences, that it could make him numb and insensible over time, wooden as a marionette doll played by strings. There was no getting around the fact that eventually he would have to "do" something with his life, and that meant finding an equivalent to little league baseball games.

So joining the military seemed like the best plan. If he needed discipline, well, that's what boot camp was for. Learn to shoot a gun straight, learn to push past pain, learn to be a winner, learn to be man. He liked it all right, at least in the beginning. His first assignment, a cruiser, didn't have enough junior officers to conn the ship so they made him an assistant navigator, and he learned how to be a conning officer. He spent a lot of time in the map room, which was always dark except for the green light that welled up through the light tables. It would glint on the officers' gold buttons and make their white shirts glow. It was beautiful, and he liked just being there, looking at the maps and helping out. They gave him a commendation medal for his work after a while, and he felt proud of himself.

But one day he made a mistake. He had a night watch, and to pass the time he started to draw in the logbook. Little doodled people dancing in around the names and times, faces with puffed out cheeks and crossed eyes blowing wind over the ledger lines like on old maps. The officer couldn't believe it when he handed it over at the end of his shift.

"You drew in the logbook?"

Jess offered to erase it.

"Erase it!?" cried the officer. "You don't erase the logbook, seaman. Nobody, but nobody, changes one goddam thing in the logbook."

The captain was even madder when he found out. He took it personally, as if a logbook on his ship with drawings in it might menace the chance for a rear admiralty he saw somewhere in his future. Jess lost his job in the map room and suffered through a long stint of dogwatches before they transferred him to another ship. He never got near a map room again.

Still, he'd been doing pretty well in the Navy. Not too long ago he even told his folks that once his tour of duty was up he'd re-enlist. When he was home on leave, he surprised himself by missing little moments on board his ship, the times he found either to hang out with his friends or be by himself. He liked going to the bow at night, way out past the guns and the paint lockers and the coils of rope. He'd smoke a cigarette and watch the boats at North Island sail past the flashing red and blue lights, and listen to the buoys gonging in the darkness. He felt attuned to his surroundings then, alive to the mystery of his presence there, as anonymous and unlikely as that might be. It was scary, how insignificant he could feel, but he had an edge, too, like the leading edge of a storm as it blows in and the air slackens, flags on flagpoles go limp, the ribbons on sailboats stop fluttering against their masts. That's how he felt, slack and breathless like that, calm before a storm.

He was only supposed to spend 48 hours in the observation ward, but on his last day one of the inmates went berserk. There was a long corridor that joined the mess hall to the open ward, and it had rows of windows on each side that looked out on the green lawns separating the wings. He was carrying his stainless-steel food tray, along with five or six others, when a guy named Jerzy stopped and said: "I wonder what'd happen if I busted out one of these windows?"

"What would happen?" Jess exclaimed, and was about to advise solemnly against it when Jerzy went ahead and put his fist through the window. Everybody froze as Jerzy examined the blood on his knuckles. It was an eerie moment, when they all seemed to be listening for the pock of God's boots on the marble floor as he came striding down the hall to punish them. Jerzy grinned grotesquely, all lit up in the sudden flush and vigor of transgression, and he put his fist through the next window over. At this point guys set down their trays and joined in on the fun. They broke out all the windows in the corridor with their fists and had a great time. Jess stood utterly bewildered, and pretty soon there was blood everywhere, spattered all over like in a slaughterhouse. Then he heard sirens and alarm bells go off, and before he could say "ratfucked," the orderlies had him and everybody else in straightjackets.

They kept him that way for 24 hours. He laid on a bunk in lockup and stared forlornly at the glaucous light welling through the fine-meshed steel grate that covered a window. That was a low point for Jess. He didn't get angry as a rule. It took a lot to ruffle the placid waters of his nature. But he was mad now, mad at those crazy fuckers in the ward, mad at himself, mad at how stupid it all was. In back of that he was scared, his heart would pound with a fear he had never felt before, a bracing sense of peril in the ordinary. There were moments in his bunk when, butterflies in his stomach, he felt so nauseated by his own helplessness that he might die of it.

Finally, a stern woman with a tired face came in and said, "I don't know who you think you are, but I'm the nurse, got it? If you mess with me when I take this straight-jacket off of you, I'll have your ass on a hotplate."

He didn't answer, just waited for her to unlace the thing and pull it off. They let him back into the open ward and the mess hall, where he kept to himself and didn't make any trouble. He stayed a few more days before they wised up and saw he didn't belong there, and then word came from the destroyer that he had to report for duty. It was set to sail for the South China Sea the next day. That morning, though, the doctor released him with a three-day chit. It was a mistake, the Marines and the Navy not interfacing the right way, but it said he didn't have to be back until Sunday. He couldn't bring himself to point this out. He took it without a word.

A while later he arrived on North Island and headed down the pier where his ship was docked. He had the job of mess cook to look forward to, the worst duty he could get. It meant staying below deck all day scraping food off plates and washing dishes. Each step closer twisted the barb of his heart even tighter. Laura O'Malley was there on the quarterdeck, logging people in. He imagined her saying, "Cooper, it's a crime not to ship out with your ship!" At the same time he thought about everything that had happened, the drug, the brig, the ward, that sense of helplessness, and he didn't care anymore. He couldn't. So he turned around and left the base, changed out of his uniform in a gas station bathroom and lighted out, officially AWOL.

2

# Josephine Street

He had no idea where to go afterward. Any friends he might turn to were either in the Navy themselves or off somewhere far away, and the prospect of checking into a hotel with nothing better to do than wander around San Diego by himself held little appeal. He also didn't want to go home, knowing his parents wouldn't understand. They'd just march him back to the base, resentful of the worry it caused them. They were nervous people and good at combining judgment with blackmail.

He did have an uncle, Milo, who lived in East Brother, a beach town up the coast a ways. He was more likely to sympathize when it came to breaking the rules. "I never put on no red tie," Jess remembered him saying once, "or went to work in a tall building. I just couldn't do it." Instead he stayed a beach bum, spent his time surfing, making art (he had a knack for it, too), and eking out a livelihood as best he could. Growing up Jess sensed he had more in common with Milo than with his mom or his dad, on some deeper level of disaffection. But his mom discouraged friendship between them, and Milo, mostly unwelcome at their house in Orange, didn't come around very often. When he did, or when they hung out on the odd occasion, they'd always hit it off. Jess, thinking he needed some of that solidarity now, headed for East Brother.

The bus he ended up taking rolled into town later that afternoon. It let him off at a stop on Del Mar Street, the festive main drag. He paused by the glass-paned shelter and looked into a bright fog for the massive trusswork of the roller coaster he knew to loom above the storefronts opposite. He only heard it—the cars as they hooked onto the cable running up the lift hill, the screams of the riders delivered over to gravity. Sound became shape, took on volume, weighed heavy like mass without matter...became vacuum, became space. He recalled his high school friend, Anselm, who played the saxophone, saying to the keyboardist in his band, "Just find a space in the music and go into it." If you closed your eyes and listened, the world would only be implied. Jess didn't have to close his eyes. Murmurous voices, the held note of a skateboard coasting down the sidewalk, the plaintive caws of crows who flew by like black newspapers adrift on a breeze. In his mind he heard a Bob Dylan song, "The Ballad of Frankie Lee and Judas Priest," and the line at the end that went: *Nothing is revealed.*

He hoisted his seabag on his shoulder and set off along Del Mar. Ghostly people wandered under the arcades, stopped in at Los Globos Taqueria, browsed the fabulous window displays of Madame Blavatsky's head-shop. At the wax museum a pirate with a three-cornered hat and an eye-patch beckoned passersby into its dim confines. "Har-har-har me matey," he repeated, his head bobbing and his good eye winking broadly at no one in particular. By the ticket counter stood a frozen highway patrolman, hand hovering open-palmed by the gun at his hip, just about to draw. Further down the street Jess passed a man on a gold lamé box, dressed entirely in gold lamé, with a gold lamé face under a gold lamé top hat, who stared so hard and still he might have been another effigy.

At a corner he turned and found himself in step with a hunched over woman about ten years older than him, with stringy black hair and glitter sprinkled around her eyes.

"You're a tall drink of water," she said conversationally. "How tall are you?"

"Six feet."

"I'm five nine."

"That's pretty tall, for a girl."

They walked on down the street, side by side.

"It's great being tall," the woman said. "People look up to you." She frowned. "Better than being short and fat. My boyfriend's short and fat. It makes him bitter. He's why I'm fat now. He complains about it. He says, 'Why are you getting so fat?' And I say, 'Whaddaya expect, when all we eat around here is chicken and chocolate?' Of course I'm gonna get fat."

Jess looked askance at her. "You're not that fat," he observed.

"I lose it pretty fast, when I set my mind to it."

They came to another corner, and still talking she peeled away down the sidewalk. "Start eating less cheese, drink non-fat milk. I slim down in no time. See you later," she said with a wave over her shoulder, off on some other tangent, toward some other chance meeting like this one not meant to last.

Jess halted, waiting for the light to change. Cars flitted past, blue and red streamers crisscrossed a car wash, and one of those revolving sidewalk signs disclosed, as if it were code, the regularly alternating words "oil" and "lube," "oil" and "lube." The fog had started burning off this far from the beach. It seemed a blue sky was about to materialize, and like the day Jess felt caught in time's skew, in the turn from what has been to what will be. He wished he could say it was a more hopeful feeling.

Once across the Pacific Coast Highway, he walked up a sloping street called Escondido, past the craftsman bungalows and clapboard carriage houses that harkened back to the early days of East Brother. The town began as an artist's colony in the late 19th century, a haven for bohemians and mystics drawn to its stretch of shoreline by the anomalous fact that it ran almost on the parallel, disorienting visitors with a sun that rose on water and set on land for much of the year. Later they built a boardwalk, which became a magnet for inland funseekers. In the twenties they built the largest wooden roller coaster in California, and with that came the merry-go-round, the Ferris wheel, the whirligig, and all the rest. The quiet artist's colony gave way to the bright lights and hectic bells of the amusement park, much to the chagrin of oldtimers whose vision of Shangri-La had taken this unexpected turn and who envied the serene glamor of the town's more reputable neighbors. East Brother has, as a result, been something of a poor relation on the south coast, known for its smoky bars, tattoo parlors, cheap motor motels, and for its populations of homeless people, sailors on leave, tourists, and other transients. With the seedy side of town more or less contained in the beach flats south of PCH, however, the rest of East Brother has shown the same prosperity as other beach towns, the same tacky art galleries, gift shops, and fancy neighborhoods winding up into the hills.

Milo lives in one of the town's first houses. His grandfather, Edwin Kreel, who owned a couple of hardware stores in Santa Ana around the turn of the last century, bought a parcel of land on the lower slopes of the hills above the Old Coast Road. When his new wife Lucy said she'd always wanted to live by the beach, he had a modest Queen Anne's cottage built for her on the property, in a style even at the time considered old-fashioned, on a mud sill foundation with lathe-and-plaster walls, a sturdy fir floor, and a wood-shingle roof. A porch ran the length of the house in front and commanded a splendid view of the undulating dunes and the topaz blue sea beyond. Lucy planted elm saplings that have since become heritage trees, and in the back, along with a rose garden, she planted a Scottish black twig apple tree grafted with Asian pears. The Kreels lived mostly in Anaheim, frequenting the house on weekends and holidays, but in 1922, during one of their visits, Edwin took off through the dunes to do some ocean fishing and dropped dead of a heart attack in the surf, where his wife, three young boys, and infant daughter found him floating like a piece of flotsam later that day.

By then neighbors had started to appear. Streets were laid down in the hills, lots graded, foundations built, house frames put in, and East Brother expanded rapidly around the first wharf at what today is the head of Calle Del Oso. After Edwin's death, Lucy moved permanently to the coast, sold off the hardware stores and raised her four children on the proceeds. She never remarried and lived on into old age to become an East Brother fixture known for her independent views and solitary character. Her sons grew up to be reliable husbands and fathers, perhaps a little too conventional to appreciate fully their mother's self-reliance, but successful enough on their own terms not to require her conformity. She never got along with her relatives, all except for her daughter Ruth and later on Ruth's two children, Milo and Jess's mom Lucille, who visited the cottage from where they lived in the Santa Ana Canyon. Milo, in particular, loved hanging out there, pottering about the yard and going down to the beach, drawing shells and seabirds into a sketchbook Lucy had given him. When Lucy died, she left the house in her will to Milo's great-uncle Roy, a sad sack of a man diagnosed with degenerative arthritis in his hip, who let the place fall into a fabulous desuetude. When he couldn't take care of himself anymore, he went to a retirement facility in Temecula and Milo, nineteen at the time, asked if he could stay in exchange for cleaning the house up, which he did with gusto, restoring it to the way he remembered it as a kid. He's lived there ever since.

Today East Brother doesn't look anything like the place Milo used to know. Development swirled up the hillsides to their very crests. On Josephine Street, where the cottage stands, Milo's watched the last vacant lots turn into homes for rich people, watched the blue grass yards go in, watched the exotic shrubs from Asia replace the salal and the manzanitas, watched the chemical annihilation of weed, vole, and slug. Only Milo and the cottage have remained more or less unchanged, each looking year by year more out of place, more anachronistic. He lets the plants around his house go wild as his neighbors groom and sculpt their yards. He lets the leaves that fall from the elm trees molder slowly into the ground rather than rake them up, and when neighbors hint casually about the importance of maintaining East Brother property values, he pretends not to understand what they're talking about.

Jess tops the hill on Escondido and turns into Josephine Street. A blue haze still shrouds the world around him. He follows the sidewalk till it stops abruptly in front of the two tall silhouetted elm trees, one on either corner of Milo's property. A thick, unkempt hedge of cypress forms an imposing rampart between and completely obscures the house from view. An opening in the hedge, high enough for a small child to walk through, is marked by a wooden mailbox and a brief unevenly stone-flagged path that leads to the front porch, plunged in gloom. Jess passes this by and walks into a dirt driveway just inside the farther elm. An orange VW Squareback is pulled up behind a derelict Datsun 510 station wagon, tucked under a mass of dark foliage. A single gable frames the second story window of a bedroom. The ridge above runs parallel to the front porch, and the roof slants like a barn to the kitchen in back. A small opened gate made of cut branches, vertically aligned, leads to a side porch enclosed within a slanting eave. At the foot of the fence is a spigot and a dirty coiled hose, a number of turned up black abalone shells fixed in a bed of soft moss, and a knee-high ceramic statue of St. Francis of Assisi with his raised hands broken off.

Jess proceeds through the gate, passing to his right the intricately tangled trunks of an evergreen tree called in Latin *euonymus Adonis*. Milo calls it the Adonis tree for short. It rises above the Datsun like a giant squid, splaying and enlacing its way laterally toward the backyard. Where the main trunk loops back on itself, Milo's driven a steel rod into the earth beneath for support. Its complicated branches thin into dense reaches of leaf and twig, touching on the eave above the porch. A subdued light gives the dark space underneath a velvety feel and limns in delicate highlights the twisted shapes of wood, the garbage cans Milo keeps there, and bicycles that lean against a fence. Next door a new house is being built right up to the property line. All Jess sees beyond is gray siding and a framed out space for a window. Someone is banging a solitary hammer in its depths.

The door is open at the side porch. Milo's kitchen is all lit up, but no one is there. A radio in another room plays faint blue notes varied and stretched to as long as four beats on a clarinet. The sound is remote and serene. A solid wood table stands just beneath the black lattice window next to the door, and against the wall at the back of the house is a sink, tiled countertops, a semi-circular glass cupboard, and a three-hob iron stove with the word "Triumph" printed on the white porcelain oven door. Against the wall opposite the side door sits a refrigerator set inside the space of an old pantry, and to the left of that are built-in shelves crammed with books.

A number of large fiberglass medallions, with painted scenes inside their scrolled frames, lie scattered about the room, propped against walls and table legs, on the floor and the counters, in the rocking chair below the book-shelves. There's a lake with chevroning geese, horseback riders on a beach, gray whales breaching, Spanish padres in brown robes and round hats, a Northwest Indian totem pole, and women in dresses sewn out of American flags exchanging gifts. They seem to have just been finished, because the smell of paint and turpentine is suffocating. The house is hot and stuffy.

Jess stands in the doorway, unsure whether to knock or holler. Just then Milo walks in from the living room, daubing a clutch of brushes with a hand towel. On see-ing Jess he starts back in sufficient fright to drop the cigarette that dangles from his mouth.

"Jesus!" he cries, anger flashing up in his eyes. "You scared me."

"I'm sorry, Milo."

"It's all right," he says, stooping for the cigarette. "I wasn't expecting you, that's all." He straightens up and takes a moment to let his racing heart slow again to nor-mal. "Come on in." He crosses to the sink. "How you doing? I thought you were in the Navy?"

"I am." Jess throws the seabag on the floor and sits on it. "I'm on leave."

"Oh." Milo puts the brushes on the counter and turns on the water. He's past fifty now, with blond hair textured like straw, leathery skin, and blue eyes a little bleached from years of too much sun. Squint lines furrow his brow and crow's feet tendril across his temples. He looks fifty the way someone who never thought he'd reach fifty might look, with surprise and disbelief woven mysteriously into the signs of age. Long practice in heedlessness to time has kept the manners of a kid pretty much intact in him. But the fact of growing old has started to catch up with him, too. It's gotten harder to avoid. His body doesn't bounce back the way it used to, his hand is less steady, and he hesitates more. Colds last longer. He can put on weight if he doesn't watch it. Right now, he's got a toothache that won't go away.

He washes his hands, staring at the orange gleam of his cigarette and his pallid reflection in the window above. He can't see the lines in his face, the strain in his eyes, but he knows they're there, looking implacably back at him.

"Why didn't you tell me you were coming?" he asks over his shoulder.

"It was kind of sudden."

Milo waits for Jess to say more, but they both end up listening to the languid clarinet on the radio in the other room.

"I was hoping I could stay for a day or two," Jess says. "If it's all right with you."

"Sure. You know you're always welcome."

There's trouble, Milo can tell. Something in the way Jess talks, dazed, cagey, scorches like a whiskey shot. He wonders why Jess isn't in his uniform. Usually, Navy guys are proud of the little customized touches they add to them—those bowties sticking way out like cat's whiskers, or pants cinched in tight at the thigh with that crisp flair at the bellbottom. But he doesn't say anything. He figures whatever the problem is will come out when it wants to. Feeling dizzy all of a sudden, he shuts his eyes to steady himself.

"Damn I hate sign painter paint," he says, on spitting the butt of his cigarette into the sink. "You gotta wash off the stuff you use to wash it off with. Even then it doesn't wash off right." He rubs his hands in the water, annoyed at the persistent greasiness between his fingers.

"You made these?"

Milo nods. "I work for a company that builds carousels. 'Special Effects,' it's called. I paint the headboards, panels, angels, things like that."

Jess looks them over. "They're good."

"They're all right," Milo says grudgingly. "I could be using acrylics, though. They're a hundred times better than this shit." Done now, he turns to face the room, drying his hands with another rag. "You get a lot more control with acrylics. If I mix chrome yellow with Prussian blue, I get light greens. If I mix mars red with yellow, I get a deep orange. I can put my blue base down and build up from there, get a nice impasto going. Plus all it's got in it is water and this plastic resin. I wouldn't have to use thinner all the time. I could wash my brushes at the kitchen sink for once."

"Why don't you use acrylics?"

"They say sign paint is more durable. I told my boss I didn't think that was true, that acrylics would last just as long in rain and sunlight as any sign painter paint. What do you see when you go downtown anyway? A lot of faded away signs, that's what. But he wouldn't listen."

Milo pulls a spindly wood chair up next to Jess and seats himself in front of a medallion. On his nose he balances a pair of glasses with only one tine and squints at the scene: two rams with swirled horns butting heads on a rocky crag. He thinks about adding volume to the cumulus clouds that catch the ambient light of a setting sun. "See that haziness in those blues and yellows?" he says, pointing. "It's almost gray. That's the sign paint. It doesn't mix well. All you get is what comes out of the can."

"It's still pretty colorful."

Milo's glad to hear that, but he frowns anyway. He can't stop thinking about how stubborn his boss is with the paint. "I guess it's the principle of the thing that bothers me," he says. "I mean, why use shitty paint with lead in it, when you can use water-based paint that glows? Why make a point of doing things ass-backward like that?"

"I don't know."

"He's that way with everything, too," Milo goes on. "Each time I suggest little improvements in the process, he says it can't be done. For instance, if it were up to me, I wouldn't paint right on the medallions like I'm doing. I'd have them made so you can insert panels inside grooves. Then I'd make these silk screens, so I'd have this stock of pictures I could print on the panels, without having to go through all this work. One of these medallions, just one, costs all told five hundred dollars. If my boss did it my way, it'd cost him two hundred. That's a three hundred dollar savings right there. He'd make a bigger profit so he could afford to pay me more, and I wouldn't have to live hand to mouth all the time. He'd be happy, I'd be happy, everybody'd be happy."

Milo moves the medallion away and puts another in its place: hounds chasing a small brown fox through the woods, with men on horses leaping over a felled tree. "It's almost like he doesn't want to be happy," he says, rolling that conundrum around in his head. "He'd rather pay more for less, take all the fun out of the work, poison his employee, and get a worse carousel for his troubles. Where's the sense in that? What do you think of that fox?"

"He's a fine fox, Milo."

"Yeah? I shouldn't make his snout longer, so he doesn't look so much like a dog?"

"He doesn't look like a dog."

"Good. I can't tell sometimes. It just becomes splotches of paint on fiberglass to me. I lose perspective."

Milo lifts out a bag of DRUM tobacco from the breast pocket in his flannel shirt. Then he pats his pants front and back, but doesn't find what he's looking for. "Be right back," he says, and scuttles off into the living room. Jess hears him tune the radio to another station. A trebly drumbeat starts up and the smooth, worried voice of Roy Orbison cuts in on the first few bars of "Blue Bayou."

Jess sees three painted carrots on the seat of the chair Milo's just left. The kitchen is full of touches like this: a bonneted mother goose hand-painted on the glass cupboard, cast-iron handles shaped like seahorses, flowers collaged out of chipped tile built into the countertops, green molding with fitted brass welding rods, faux-grained cabinet doors, and a trompe l'oeil shelf atop the bookcase, with baize green and red leather volumes tilted upright or piled on their sides.

Milo likes these details. He spends time on them. Jess doesn't know anybody else who does that. His parents don't, that's for sure. Their ranch house in Orange is nice enough, but there's nothing unique about it, nothing that reveals the passions of the people who live there, unless fear can be a passion. That does sort of tie everything together: framed Renoir posters under glass, lace antimacassars, plastic runners on the carpets, air purifiers in every room. Hygiene is what his mom and dad mean by care. Jess remembers his mom saying Milo didn't care about anything, and the proof for her, apart from the fact he never amounted to something she could respect or envy, was how slovenly he kept house. It's true, his house is a mess. The walls are stained yellow and there's cobwebs in the corners. Things feel pretty rundown. But her judgment always seemed unfair to Jess, the product of a secret inflexibility that bothered him because she would never admit to what it was: clinging to a version of life that belonged only to her and not to other people. For some reason she needed to be hard that way to get through.

Milo returns with his rolling papers, sits at the table this time, and begins rolling another cigarette. "Been drawing lately?"

"Not much."

"The Navy keeps you busy, I bet." He lays the tobacco out on the paper and rubs it between his fingers.

"I have time enough. Somehow I don't get around to it."

"Why not, if you like it?"

"I don't know. I do like it. I just don't do it."

Milo senses evasion in this, even though he knows what his nephew's talking about. It's hard to do what you like doing. This world doesn't like you to do what you like, and it's hard to clean latrines for eight hours and come home expecting to be anything but a zombie. Milo's spent his life in full retreat from that scenario. Sometimes it's worked, sometimes it hasn't. There's been some pretty lean years, times when he had no choice but to hire himself on at construction sites so he could bang nails, twist wire, and mix concrete for ten dollars an hour. But mostly he's managed to find his détentes with the work world, to keep himself steady on the path of arts and crafts. He's done everything from paint pictures on surfboards and the sides of vans to make mobiles out of driftwood and shells to sell on Del Mar Street. It hasn't been easy, maybe in the end it hasn't kept him from bitterness and regret, but at least he's been able to do what he likes. He's never been rich, mostly he's been pretty damn poor, and he can't say it's been as much fun as he wanted it to be, but all in all he can't complain.

"Seems to me you gotta do it anyway," he tells Jess, licking the end of the paper and bringing the tobacco into a cylinder. "If you don't put up a fight, they're gonna beat you down into what they want. And what they want is a draft horse, a camel, somebody to do their work for them."

"The problem is I don't feel like fighting when I feel like drawing."

"What are you talking about?!" Milo cries. "If that was true, you'd never do it." He pinches the excess tobacco from one end of the reefer and lights the other. A hood of smoke drifts up around his head. He decides his nephew needs some setting straight. "Art's not this ethereal dream people think it is," he explains. "It's hard, objective, like building a house: you start by laying down a chalk line in the dirt. People don't understand that. Hell, they don't even understand it when they're building a house! They say, 'I want a house with seven stories and no stairs, cork floors, mobile walls, and a flying roof made out of styrene foam.' 'Well, you can't have that,' I tell them. 'I can't?' 'No, but you can have this ordinary frame house with two bedrooms upstairs and a deck off the living room and kitchen downstairs, if you want.'"

"I always wanted high ceilings," admits Jess, "and big windows, like in a warehouse."

"There you go," says Milo disdainfully. "Pretty soon you want enough space to shuttle a few clouds back and forth. Pretty soon you want an all-glass house suspended like a bubble out over the ocean, or some shit like that."

Milo feels the irritation that prefigures one of his rants on art and artists. They come over him now and then. He's been on a crusade for a long time against modern art. Navel gazing, he calls it. Pouring honey on the ground and dropping acorns on it. Smearing mayonnaise all over your body and masturbating in the town square. That's not art! Nobody knows what it means. Nobody recognizes themselves in it. It's not about building a community or even reminding people of the eternal verities, cosmic balance, the miracle of those films we are, stretched over infinite night. All art means these days is vainglory, in Milo's view, and he's tired of vainglory, his or anyone else's. He wants to cut honestly to the bone now, to the work stored up in things like marrow.

"Don't let anybody tell you art's ethereal," he advises Jess. "They're lying to you. It's hard. It's real. It's not 'that's a picture of a goose.' It's 'that's a goose. That's my goose. I was trying to say goose there...'"

On this note he finds himself ranging back through all the accumulated disappointments of his life as an artist, through all those times he drew a goose and showed it to people and they thought it was a duck. Man, it hurts when people don't understand what you're trying to say, or share. And not only because of the failure. He can take that, hard as it is. It's more because of the modern world, where anything can be art and anybody can be an artist, but nothing has any value and nobody understands one another. People can't agree on even the most basic things. It's all the same. Duck, goose, fox, dog. Nothing matters. No one cares. That's what hurts.

"Craft is the word I'm looking for," he says. "There's no craftsmanship in art anymore. It doesn't require skill. In fact, people who have skill aren't considered artists. Even a bitchin' artist like Norman Rockwell is looked down on these days. I like Norman Rockwell, I can't help it. And I'm sick of being told how all those scenes he painted of people leading happy lives were somehow bad. They weren't bad. Happiness isn't bad. He was just a sincere guy painting pictures of people the way he wanted to. He wasn't cynical about it. That's the difference. I won't let anybody tell me there can't be some innocence in the world...."

Milo falters, doubtful all of a sudden. It occurs to him that his values have no more weight than anything else, if he's right. When nothing matters, the perception that nothing matters doesn't matter either. It scatters like spindrift on the beach of the modern world, where he goes looking for ineffaceable tracks. The problem is there aren't any. All the traces of people who've come before vanish in the wind, leaving no path to follow, no insoluble past, only a present confusion. Is there no innocence in the world? he asks himself. Worse, is the desire for innocence only another kind of cynicism? Is happiness, in fact, bad? He wants to be decisive now, push ahead on that beach, know where he's going, find what he believes in like a turban shell by the ethereal sea, but each effort only folds him more deeply into trackless space, into East Brother time, into the growing suspicion that life's a big and tasteless joke and all Milo knows about it is that somehow it's on him.

Jess sits by, silent and patient, as Milo broods. He's noticed before how his uncle goes into his own internal world. He ends up talking in monologues a lot. Jess doesn't mind. He's always known how to be alone with people, how to wait for them to make their way through the thing they can't stop thinking about. Jess's way of going inside is different. He might be just as torn up about some problem, like he is now, but he doesn't bring it out or share it. He almost can't. The words never come. The time never seems right. Instead he falls into a trance, tunes in at very subliminal frequencies, like a hibernating animal.

They listen to the radio for a while. Milo floats on the dark tide of his presentiments, letting its swollen current carry him away to other metaphors. He says: "You ever walk into a room and sense there were things going on you had no idea about? And that you weren't ever going to have any idea about? I've been sensing that a lot lately. It's like I'm in a room I'm not supposed to be in, and everybody's playing a game I don't know the rules for. No matter how hard I try, I can't shake the feeling that I'm an interloper."

"I used to feel that way in school," Jess recalls. "Like I'm not supposed to be there, but I am supposed to be there, too. I'm supposed to feel like I'm not supposed to be there."

There's a knock at the front door. Milo ignores it. "You're an interloper," he says. "People look at you like you've done something wrong, only the thing you've done wrong is be yourself. It's not what you've done but who you are that's wrong."

The knock comes again.

"I hate that," Milo says. "Because I don't want life to be a game. I want it to be real. So I can say, 'this life's like getting high and it'll wear off after a while. I'm gonna go over and step in front of that white Ford.' Soon as I do and it runs me down, I'll hear the voices of people at some party, laughing and shouting."

"There's somebody at your front door," says Jess.

"I know." He doesn't want to answer it. "If it's not somebody who knows I let people in at the side door, it's nobody I care to see."

Right then a woman with long angled blond hair appears on the porch.

"Hellooo!" she sings out.

Milo gets up gruffly and jerks open the door. "Yeah?"

The woman wears a lemon-yellow polyester dress suit with lacy lapels, open at the throat. Her face is caked with makeup, her lips bright red, and her eyes blink gamely beneath lashes laden thick with mascara. Her pursed expression is every inch as tense and unsure as Milo's. For a second they mirror each other. She steals a glance over Milo's shoulder, taking in the room and Jess.

"Are you Mr. Manning?"

"That's right."

"My name is Stacey Livingston," she says, holding out her hand. When he doesn't shake it, she balls her fingers into a fist. "I represent Contempo Realty right here in East Brother, Mr. Manning."

"Contem*po*?"

"Contem*po*," she echoes. "We were wondering if we might, well, chat a little about your lovely home—"

"Who's we?"

"What?"

"Am I going to be chatting with you, or are there others?" Milo enunciates.

The woman decides to ignore this. "Those of us at Contempo have had our eye on your home for quite some time now."

"Uh-huh."

"Do you realize," she leans in seductively, a keen scent of perfume wafting through the room, "how much your home would be worth on today's market, given its central location right here in the middle of beautiful East Brother?"

"No."

"Well, if you will allow me," she says, pawing at a leather briefcase, "we'd like to inform you of the opportunity you have right now to sell your home for a price impossible to imagine even a few years ago."

"I'm not interested—"

"I have a fact sheet for you to look at—"

"I said I'm not interested."

She still didn't hear him. "We can't tell you how exciting a time it is to be in real estate."

"I don't care how exciting a time it is to be in real estate. Fuck real estate."

"With appreciation rates at record highs—"

"Get out of here!" barks Milo.

"And interest rates that are very favorable to homeowners—"

"I said get the fuck out!" Startled, she takes a step back from the door.

"Mr. Manning!"

"I'm sick of you people harassing me," Milo grouses. "I ain't gonna sell my house, period."

"We just thought you'd like to know what your options are."

"I don't want to know what my options are!"

"We only have your best interests at heart—"

"What are you talking about? The only interests you know are your own. And they're not in your heart."

This gets Ms. Livingston's back up. "Contento has the finest reputation of—"

"I thought you said Contempo?"

"I did." She gulps, blushing furiously.

"I knew it," says Milo. "I fucking knew it. Contento sent you. You tell that sonofabitch this is war. If I see one more of his evil-assed minions around here, I shoot to kill, you hear me?"

"Be reasonable, Mr. Manning," she urges, Milo meanwhile producing a .410-gauge shotgun from a closet in the hallway and cocking the external hammer. "...Mr. Manning...?"

He takes aim at her face. "Aaagggghhhh!" She whips around the corner out of sight. They listen to the thud of her fleeing footfalls in the driveway.

"Fucking snake," growls Milo, stepping onto the porch and peering around the corner to make sure she's gone. "Rattlesnake." He comes back in. "Did you know a rattlesnake can kill you even when it's dead? A rattlesnake can kill you even when it's been cut in half. Even twenty-four hours later."

"Is that gun loaded?"

"It's got a slug of double ought buckshot in it. It's probably been there for forty years, but it's there."

"Who's Contento?"

"A real estate agent," Milo says. "And my nemesis. For years he's been trying to sell my house out from under me. I don't let him near the place anymore, so he sics people like her on me instead."

"Why does he want to sell your house?"

"It's personal. He hates me." Milo puts the gun away again. "Plus everybody wants to live here. Millionaires want to live here. I've got millionaires for neighbors. I'm living like a church mouse while the guy next door's building his summer home with eight bedrooms and a ten-car garage."

He sits in his wonted chair before the small color television on his kitchen table and one more time tries to settle jangled nerves. It's getting late. The light in the windows turns almost blue in the mist, robin's egg blue, washed like blue watercolor on a page. Spiderwebs glow in the windowsills, and you can see the careful, precise movements of the spider's legs as they pluck the silky strings. Moths appear outside, fluttering helplessly against the glass. He fishes out a piece of scratch paper from the miscellaneous pile of change, receipts, cigarette butts, guitar picks, disemboweled mechanical pencils, cubes of wax, an airbrush nozzle, and a rusted caliper on the table, and edgily starts to draw a cormorant standing on a rock. He's a cormorant standing on the rock of his exasperation now, and it's called real estate. There isn't anything real about real estate, he silently opines.

"They got a lot of nerve thinking I'd sell my grandmother's house," he says. "I might as well sell my grandmother. Shit. I'd rather burn the place down than hand it over to the likes of Harry Contento." He squints at his cormorant, shading its hieroglyphic body with a rapid oscillation of his hand. Through another long pause his thoughts shift to other things fiery. "Once, when I was a kid," he recollects, "I had a 1928 Chevy pickup that was stripped to the frame. All the fenders and doors and chrome, stripped off. Only the cowling was left, and the seats. It burned up in a brush fire, which just about killed me. I loved that old car. But I was glad for it, too, in a way, because at least then nobody else got to have it. 'Nope,' I said at the time. 'Better this way. Let it burn.'"

Jess, now seated at the table, has been absorbed in the reflections on the window by his shoulder. Slowly he realizes that a man is standing behind the pane, staring back at him from under a Panama hat the way a buzzard might eye a squashed rabbit. It seems he's been there a while, waiting for his chance to move in on the feast. Upon detection, however, he raps the window with his knuckles.

"Jack the Cat!" he cries. "Jack the Cat!"

Milo opens the door on a man about his age, who sidles in with a chunk of smooth colored glass in one hand. He nods at Jess, sits down at the table, and says: "Guess what?"

"What?" says Milo

He beams. "I'm down to twenty-seven grams today!"

"No kidding? Congratulations."

"Thanks," he says. "The only problem is, I just had my take home privileges suspended."

"Jess. This is Jack."

"How's it going," Jack says, without looking at him.

"Fine."

"That's too bad," resumes Milo.

"Too bad?!" cries Jack. "It's terrible. I'm trapped! I can't leave East Brother. I gotta be at the clinic by eight in the morning every fucking day. Before, I could stay away two, three, maybe four days straight. I'd ration the methadone to make it last a week even, sell a day's worth for ready cash, and take off for LA or Vegas. But I went in the other day, and the nurse—Nurse Ratshit I call her—saw a sixteenth of an inch in my cup and knew I was rationing it. Bam! Automatic two-month suspension and probation."

"You're not on a maintenance program to get off heroin, Jack, but to stay on methadone."

"Right, right." He glances around the room. "Why's it so hot in here?"

"I'm drying my paintings."

"It stinks," he says, wrinkling his nose. "Solvents, man. Bad stuff. Get them under your fingernails or in your skin, and they go straight to your liver."

"How's the glass business going?" Milo says, with an obligatory tone that his friend doesn't catch. Jack's most recent scheme has been to gather discarded fragments of glass from a lamp factory in East Brother and turn them into collectibles. He tumbles them or heats them to pour into molds and sells them as curios, paperweights, magic talismans, objects of divination, anything he can think up or people want. He was doing fairly well until his wife Moira divorced him and took away the business in one fell legal swoop. Now he's had to start from scratch.

"It's coming along," he says. "No take-home privileges is slowing things down, but my luck's definitely changing. I met this guy who's maybe interested in the turtles and frogs. I'm also making these holders for votive candles. Churches'll snap those up. And then there's talk of putting glass dust in these wands with stars on top of them. They have liquid inside, so when you shake them, the glass swirls around. I figure in a few months I stand to make thirty to forty grand just from that."

"Uh-huh."

"It won't be for a few months, though, and in the meantime I got nothing coming in."

"Uh-huh." Milo's heard this sort of off-handed qualification before.

"I brought this for you, by the way," he says, holding up the chunk. "You can keep it."

"Thanks."

"It's only a matter of time," Jack says confidently, "before I get back to where I was last year. My lawyer's working on Moira, and he thinks I can get the fish contract back. The crystals and shit, no way, that's gone. But I get the fish tanks."

"You sell this?" Jess asks, pointing at the chunk.

"Stuff like it, yeah." He hands it over. "Feel how heavy that is."

Jess hefts it.

"You know what you're holding there?" Jack says. "An empire, that's what. I had an empire made out of this shit. And I was emperor, until my wife staged a coup d'état."

He slumps sideways in his chair. Suddenly he looks tired. A savage experience plays into his still handsome face. To Jess he seems both youthful and ancient beyond years, like some bedraggled angel but lately escaped from the storm of time, hardly able to close his wings.

"Women," sighs Jack with an exasperated lift of the brow. "My luck always changes when a woman comes around. My luck really changed with my first wife, Hippolyta." He rolls his eyes in awe at her august and diabolical memory. "Before her, I could always count on that magical something to come through for me. Remember those early days, Milo? The smugglers were dropping so much dope they lost five or six bales a day practically. I was pulling down ten grand a month just on what they wrote off. Of course," he checks himself, "I never did make that much since I was paying for a 1,200 dollar a week habit, but that was the beginning, the days of innocence and faith, when everything I did turned out right."

Milo asks Jess if he'd like spaghetti and meat sauce for dinner. Jess nods.

"I'd go to the Virgin Islands," says Jack nostalgically, "or over to San Juan, Puerto Rico, and gamble. In half an hour I'd make a hundred grand. I'm not kidding. I'd be high, and I'd be thinking 12s and snake eyes, throwing the dice and rolling 12s every time. It was the weirdest thing. The first twenty minutes on dope I could always win. My problem was I stayed, cuz half an hour later I lost it all again."

"What were you doing in the Caribbean?" asks Jess. That's one place he's never been, belonging as he does to the Pacific fleet.

"Had business down there, in this old fort, or slum really, with gambling, drugs, a lot of cargo running through. It was quite a place. Malparaiso. 'Bad Paradise.'" He grins to himself, remembering. "Go in there you got ocean views, hookers grabbing at your wrists"—he grabs Jess's wrist—"people packing ounces of cocaine in their pockets, smoking spliffs with the spit of the fucking Jamaica on them. Those were the days."

"That was before your luck changed," adds Milo, ruefully banging around in cupboards for pots and pans.

"Right," says Jack. "But even afterward, when I lived there again, it wasn't so bad. The place was crawling with dope. They had more dope than food. In St. Croix, during Hurricane Hugo, the people revolted, right. You know why? Because they didn't have any food. All they had was cocaine, millions of dollars' worth of cocaine. They were starving to death, and all they could do was get high."

Jess watches Jack intently, not sure whether it's his imagination, or whether there really is a halo shimmering around his opaque figure. He might be about to vanish in it.

"People lived and breathed dope down there," Jack goes on. "Once I went to the doctor in Charlotte Amalie because I hurt my back, thinking I'd get Percodans or something. The guy gives me five *hundred* morphine pills. Or listen to this: I was living in a shack, with no money, off the heroin for the first time in my life, down on my luck, man, I mean down on my ass-breaking luck, and I notice this shrub growing all around the place, with little bell-shaped leaves and black berries. 'What's that?' I ask and somebody tells me, 'man, that's belladonna.' Belladonna!" Jack cries, waiting in Jess for the little signs of recognition this word should inspire, but not finding them. "There ain't nothing like belladonna, let me tell you. That stuff'll kill you. Never take the seeds or you're a dead man. Only take the leaves. I was a belladonna junkie in no time."

Jess wonders if this is what Jack means by good luck or bad luck, but he sees no opportunity to ask which it might be, since Jack leaves little room in general for interruption. Milo lights the gas burners on the stove and sets the water boiling.

"The first twenty minutes on heroin," says Jack, nodding in the fond memory of old nods, "are the best. There's nothing like it. Everybody should try it. In fact, they should make it legal."

"Jack," says Milo.

"What?"

Milo glances at Jess. He doesn't want his uptight sister accusing him of turning her son into a heroin addict.

"I mean," says Jack, catching on, "they should make it legal, but only if you're forty. That should be the heroin age. No one under forty should be allowed to shoot, smoke, sniff, free base, or otherwise fuck with the opium leaf. Like in the Middle East. Over there old people are always chewing on opium leaves. But only the old people."

There's a pause. Jack grabs at a paper bag on the table, pries it open, and looks inside. He sticks his whole face deep in the bag and sniffs. "You get a buzz from this shit, Milo?"

"A little."

"It's nothing but twigs and seeds."

"That's right."

"Don't I owe you an eighth, or a quarter, or something?"

"I kinda thought it was a half, Jack."

"A half?" he says incredulously. "No way. Couldn't be."

He puts the bag down and casts around for something to do, but nothing presents itself. He's fishing for an invitation to dinner, and Milo knows it.

"Save those seeds," he tells him. "Don't throw those away. They're gold. You ever take morning glory seeds?"

"Can't say as I have," says Milo.

"How about you?" He looks hard at Jess, who shakes his head.

"They're okay. A shot glass of morning glory seeds. But they ain't nothing compared to belladonna."

"Why do you call yourself Jack the Cat?" Jess asks.

"I've got nine lives."

"At least," chimes in Milo.

"You don't look like a cat."

"Don't tell me!" cries Jack. "I look like a bird."

"A bird?" says Jess, that image of an angel duly shifting in his mind. He still got to keep his wings.

"That's what everybody says, that I'm bird-like, and that if I was a cat, I'd eat myself."

"So it's because you're lucky that they call you Jack the Cat?"

"Man, I could tell you stories you wouldn't believe," says Jack. "Some of the things I've been to the other side and back of would blow your fucking mind."

Jess, grateful for the relief he was finding in the two men's company and glad he'd hit on the idea of coming to East Brother, is interested. Milo's not. He's tired of Jack's dope stories. As rollicking as they might be, they're always the same, kernels of truth surrounded by lies and exaggeration, and every time the lies are different, every time that kernel undergoes slightly more exaggeration, till you can't tell anymore what's true, or if anything is true.

The spaghetti's in the pot, and he's cooking onions and hamburger meat in a skillet. At length he adds in a bottle of tomato sauce. A head of broccoli steams in a second pot. He takes out plates and forks. When he sets them on the table, all eyes following him, he says, "How's about staying for dinner, Jack?"

To which Jack replies: "You got something to drink, a beer maybe?"

"No," Milo says. "No beer."

"Oh. Maybe I'll roll a reefer of this shake. Is that okay?"

"Sure."

Milo gets glasses and a plastic bottle of cranberry juice from the refrigerator. The windows are dusky now. The warm light of the kitchen gains in luster by the contrast. Bugs bob at the ceiling. The smell of the sauce seeps into the linseed oil, turpentine, and marijuana smoke, forming in the hothouse of the room a thick olfactory mulch. Milo opens the square window beside the stove, built into the space of an old vent that used to be part of a cold storage cabinet. Above him, on a shelf that runs by the ceiling from the corner to the cupboard with a hand-painted goose on the pane, old wall clocks and mantel clocks look out with their bull's eye glass dials in brown sashes, their pendulums and gongs, their dead barometers and thermometers, and none of them tells the right time. He hears the intricate mandolin and fiddle tessitura of a blue grass song on the radio. It makes him long for, well, something hard to name, something natural—a musty smell, worn supple leather, glow worms in orange groves, dried butterflies that turn to powder at the touch. In this wistful feeling he transfers the cooked spaghetti to a bowl and pours the bubbling sauce over it, then carries the bowl to the table and heaps spaghetti onto the plates. He adds the broccoli, puts salt and pepper shakers on the table, and sits down to listen with his nephew to the incredible story of Jack the Cat.

3

# Dope Story

Jack the Cat found himself ringleader of East Brother's largest drug smuggling operation more by design than accident. Life was like that. Events never quite took him by surprise, which was to say they always surprised the hell out of him, but with this sneaking suspicion that it was all part of some cosmic pattern. Nothing was haphazard because everything had happened before, his life had come and gone countless times, Jack the Cat was as old as the winds.

Jack Wind, in fact, he would later make an alias, out of respect for the providential feeling he'd had ever since he was Jack Milich, only kid of Slovenian ancestry in an all-Italian neighborhood of New York's Lower East Side and scared out of his head. It would take him a long time to figure out he was not like other mortals, but an early sign would be turning eighteen without once having been beat up, stabbed, or shot for not being Italian.

With this scrap of benediction to go by, he moved to California, Lotus Land, El Dorado, Mahagonny, where, like so many others, he hoped to make his mark. Success didn't come over night. He bounced up and down the coast for a few years, causing small wonders to occur here and there, but nothing extraordinary enough to suggest how charmed he really was. When he arrived in East Brother, looking for all the world like just another beach bum living in ramshackle bungalows behind the surf shops on Del Mar Street, no one would have said that there went the mastermind of a veritable drug empire, least of all Jack the Cat.

Down as he may have been, however, he still kept an eye out for changes in fortune. Alertness of this kind came easy to him, the consequence of a well-honed instinct he had for taking advantage of a situation, whatever it might be and wherever it might develop. It was in the grip of this instinct, walking off a hangover on a solitary stretch of East Brother Beach one morning before dawn, that he found five bales of Colombian gold washed up by the sea stack off Calle Santa Maria.

His first thought was how to get the bales to his bungalow without attracting notice. He lived a mile away as the crow flies, and the bales weighed about seventy pounds each wet, so he'd clearly need a truck. But as it was against the law to drive a truck onto the sand and he didn't have one anyway, his other option was to lug each bale in plain sight back across the beach, up the stairs and around the boardwalk, along Del Mar Street and down the alley to his place. He did this three times before he saw anybody, but on the fourth trip the usual contingent of surfers, joggers, beachcombers, and tai chi devotees started populating the level sands. Cars cruised by in slow motion up on West Cliff Drive. Street people stirred in their sleeping bags by the Promenade. On Del Mar, meter maids tweaked the meters and the liquor stores opened.

After stashing that fourth bale in his closet, he sprinted back to the beach to find two six-year-olds poking at the last one.

"Hey!" he cried. "Leave my package alone. Get away from there."

"What's in it?" one of the kids asked.

"My life," said Jack the Cat. "My whole life, that's what."

"You just come ashore with it?" the other kid asked.

"That's right," he said, flustered. "That's right, I've been living in the sea. I'm a fucking sea monster, and I don't like curious kids either, except to eat. Get out of here!"

He carried the last bale with all the nonchalance he could muster, whistling the Eddie Arnold tune "Cattle Call" as he imagined an ordinary citizen might on an ordinary stroll, and reached the sanctuary of his door like an escaped convict the threshold of a monastery.

His first impulse—or, rather, his second, since the first thing he did was roll a joint of the smooth, well-cured weed and smoke it—was to get out there selling the stuff right away. He knew by the immediate sedative effect that he was in possession of premium buds and that the sky was the limit as far as price was concerned. He didn't get too far in this line of reasoning, though, before the dope's power announced itself like free fall on a roller coaster ride. When he got up from that he was leery enough to know he'd better think twice before introducing this shit to the streets, since whoever it belonged to was going to know it when they smoked it.

That's what his friend Milo said. "Man, you can't do nothing with pot like this," he advised that evening, stoned on Jack the Cat's floor. "It'd be like sending up a flare in this desert of low-grade dope."

"What am I gonna do?" cried Jack the Cat. "A find like this doesn't happen every day, and for a guy like me not selling it's like telling a peacock he can't preen."

"Give it back," said Milo. "Find out whose it is and give it back. Minus a stash for yourself, of course. Nobody, no matter how cutthroat, would expect you not to get some reward."

So that's what Jack the Cat tried to do. He didn't want any trouble with big-time criminals, guys who'd kill you for a lot less than 250 pounds of Colombian gold, and he never once considered himself a player in his own right. The problem was he couldn't find out who it belonged to. No rumors surfaced on the streets. Nobody responded to the carefully coded inquiries he made to those in the know. This went on for a week, and by the end of it Jack the Cat was a wreck. He couldn't sell the stuff, and he couldn't not sell it. He couldn't even give it away.

"Maybe it doesn't belong to anybody?" he asked hopefully of Milo.

"Are you crazy? Shit like this always belongs to somebody. That's the American Way. There ain't no such thing as miracles."

Jack the Cat didn't know exactly what Milo meant by that, but since he spoke with conviction, and Jack the Cat's nerves, frayed by then to impressionable dendrites, fibrillated polyrhythmically, he accepted it as true.

"What am I going to do?"

"Turn it in," said Milo.

"Turn it in!" he gasped.

"Give it to the cops. It's the safest thing. Just say you found it on the beach."

The idea of relinquishing thousands of dollars worth of premium dope offended every principle Jack lived by. "I have never willingly walked into no fucking police station," he averred, picking one, "and I'm not about to change my ways now."

"Just call them up," said Milo. "Soon as you explain to them what it is and that you want to turn it in, they'll come here and get it."

He called the next morning. The words stuck in his throat. Behind his eyes, unaccountably, he had a vision of hundred-dollar bills swirling like confetti down Fifth Avenue.

"Yeah, well, listen, I found these five bales of...well, marijuana, and, yeah, like, I thought you guys...I mean, guys and gals, might want to...know about it."

"Is that a fact?" said the lady. "I'm sure my superiors will be interested to hear that, and I'll relay the news to them as soon as I can. Thank you for calling."

She hung up.

Fifth Avenue vanished from Jack's mind, and those hundred-dollar bills turned into helixes of stringy light corkscrewing through a dark void. He lost his balance and staggered back into Milo's arms.

"What happened?" said Milo.

"She hung up on me."

"She hung up?"

"Yeah."

"She didn't take down your name even?"

"Nothing, man."

Milo told him to call her back.

"Listen, lady," he said, "I don't think you understand me. I got here 250 pounds of the finest grade Colombian gold cannabis indica that money can buy."

"That is rather a coup," she said tartly. "Maybe you should talk to Sergeant Donner."

"Hello!" said a man's voice, and Jack the Cat told him about it. "You do?" he said. "That's something. That is something. Look, I got in my hand a piece of paper they call a police report. What I'm going to do is file one of these babies away here and get back to you. How does that sound?"

More like it, that's what. For another week Jack the Cat rested easy. Aside from the usual needling scruples of a man of his caliber, he almost convinced himself that all was for the best. Jack the Cat was lucky once again in the humble way he'd grown accustomed to settling for. He even looked forward to getting rid of the dope.

After two weeks with no word, however, fear began to creep back. When the silence stretched to a month, Jack the Cat could regularly be seen quaking pale and hollow-eyed down Del Mar Street. He couldn't hold a cigarette without trembling, and his voice broke into a thin haunted squeal at the mere sight of a police officer, often when his friends were modulating the conversation to a discreet whisper.

Milo urged him to call Sergeant Donner again.

"Oh yes, I recall," the sergeant said. "Retrieved a little detritus from the beach, or something to that effect. Decent of you. Do we want it? Now what would a police station want with a thing like that? Are you insinuating something?"

"No," said Jack the Cat, "I'm just trying to do my..." He paused.

"Civic duty," Milo hissed at him.

"Civic duty," he duly pronounced.

"I don't like the tone of your voice, mister," the sergeant snapped. "I think you're one of those people who don't think too highly of law enforcement. Is that true? What do you think would happen to that nice tidy little home and that nice tidy little wife you got tucked away on some cul-de-sac somewhere, if we weren't out patrolling the streets, keeping the lowlifes in line, booting them out of your neighborhood at night? Anarchy, that's what! Without the man in uniform the streets of East Brother would look like a jungle, Jack, so don't go talking to me about no civic duty. If you did your goddam civic duty, you'd stay in your goddam fancy-assed house and stop bothering us down here, who have work to do!"

The line went dead. Milo, who heard this harangue from across the room, was completely dumbfounded. That wasn't the way policemen talked! He railed at the universe, inquired of higher powers if it was or was not true that they were in the midst of a war on drugs, and rolled himself a reefer the better to attune himself to any answers that might be coming down the pike. Jack the Cat, meanwhile, stood by the phone pensively. He was beginning to think the cops didn't want anything to do with his five bales and that he shouldn't be so surprised by this. Maybe it was time to accept that things just didn't happen for him the same as they did to other people. He had some sort of special dispensation. Destiny was his lot, his portion in life. Realism was just a way of denying reality.

The next morning about fifteen cops busted in his door. They produced a warrant to search the residence of one Jack Small for any illegal narcotics or narcotics paraphernalia. "We know you're the biggest drug dealer in East Brother," they said on proceeding to tear the place apart.

Jack the Cat had to laugh. "Me?" he cried. "I'm small-fry, man. Low-echelon hustler. You should go after that guy who keeps saying he's got five bales of Colombian hash. Now he's a fucking gangster."

The cops left no cellophane wrapper, eye dropper, bottle cap, salt shaker, or bunsen burner unturned, but in the end they came up empty since Jack the Cat had taken the precaution of moving the bales over to Milo's place. This, however, like the search itself, had stamped on it the irrelevance of something already decided, a procedure done for the sake of appearance, nothing more. "I'm sure glad we got you guys protecting our streets from the riff-raff," said Jack the Cat boldly, the cops filing back out the door again. "I sleep better because of it, believe me."

That was the beginning of a new era in law enforcement-Jack the Cat relations: they never bothered him again. He started selling his stash in small sums but steadily widening markets, raking in so much money he couldn't spend it fast enough, except to buy more dope. Dope started producing more dope almost at once. Problem was, the stuff he bought wasn't so exotic as the Colombian gold. North Coast sensimilla, Big Sur holy weed, local shit that was half stems and seeds—selling this stuff put him in competition with everybody else, and he liked being a player a lot more than he even thought he would.

How to expand on the supply side of things became a priority as the fabled five bales dwindled and his popularity in beach flat circles started returning to pre-windfall levels. He needed a fresh infusion of capital and more reliable sources, but for the life of him he couldn't see how to finagle either, short of another miracle. Toward this end he took to walking along the beach at night to see the dawn come on, hoping the ocean might disgorge another shipment or two for his private delectation. He knew it was a desperate act. Chance never worked the same way twice. It had to be helped along, encouraged. Fatalism was an art form, and luck only half the equation. The other half was craft, or cunning; without that, he was just another amateur. Pretty soon he'd be back to where he started, if not to where he belonged: loitering by the arcades and muttering to passersby "buds, buds, doses, tender green buds?" along with Milo and all the rest.

To such dejection had this dismal prospect reduced him that he just assumed he was crazy when he started noticing blue lights on the water, during those late-night walks down the beach. Light shows were hardly infrequent for Jack the Cat. He was used to living on that fringe where phenomena winked uncertainly back at him. At first he ignored them, then he obsessed about them, then he settled in to a bad faith that balanced out despair and mania pretty well. Blue lights, blue lights splattering in the verge of white surf, glittering like sapphires, like fallen stars, like the eyes of dead pirates who had to become insurance salesmen when business dried up. Fuck, man.

It came as quite a shock, then, when his girlfriend, who answered to the name Janet Greendorfer when she was running the East Brother Lifeguard Training School but was otherwise known in beach flat circles as Queen Hippolyta on account of her regal 6'3" stature, accompanied him on the beach one morning after a night of vigorous debauchery and said with casual intonation,

"See those blue lights out there?"

Jack the Cat looked up to her. She was gorgeous even in the dark, a leopard and a lioness crossed, with a blonde mane and shoulders thrust back like the winged Nike of Samothrace. He considered whether whimpering was a good idea in front of a goddess like that.

"What blue lights?" he said hopelessly. "I don't see no blue lights."

"Out there," she said, "flickering on the water."

He turned to the dark horizon as it slowly split the night. Horror spread in him. There were the blue lights of ferries crossing over Jack's River Styx, and Hippolyta could see them, too. Fuck. She'd be gone inside of a week, he predicted—back to the likes of Moley Foley, surf champion for two years running and first-class musclehead, or Gid Boone, master boatbuilder and ex-NFL star who placed in last year's Hornblower Yacht Race to Hawaii.

"You know what they are?" said Hippolyta.

"Those blue lights?"

"Yeah."

My doom, he said to himself. My miserable, awful, heinous, and execrable doom. He had an urge to kiss her one last time before it was too late.

"They're buoys," she said.

"Boys?"

"Bu-oys." They both listened to the pounding of the surf.

"What kind of buoys?"

"The kind drug smugglers use."

"Drug smugglers?" cried Jack the Cat imperiously. "Drug smugglers? What drug smugglers?"

"I don't know who they are, stupid. They come in boats, and drop their shipments at night so they sink under these buoys. And the buoys have these little blue lights on them, so whoever it is that picks them up can find them again. Moley told me."

Jack the Cat's brow went arching right about up to the moon when he heard this, and not even the mention of Moley's name could shake him free from a weird tingling in the bones.

But that was nothing compared to the awe he felt in the boat with Milo one night later, pulling up the blue-lighted buoy to discover a cargo of high-grade uncut heroin in an airtight container with the phrase "The Devil Is a Transporter" printed on the lid. When those words swam up out of the water into the beam of his flashlight, Jack broke out in giddy tears. He laughed at Milo's jumpy fear of getting caught. He danced over tackle boxes and fishing nets. He looked up at the star-encrusted sky and humbly thought how grand it all was, poking himself to make sure he wasn't tripping.

The next phase in his empire building began that night, its diversification into the heady markets of cocaine and heroin smuggled by sea into East Brother. In the beginning he intercepted cargoes selectively, choosing those that, by some criterion of his own unholy devising, might be considered legitimate salvage. He expected wrath and retribution to descend upon him hourly, of course, but no nameless kingpin appeared, no outlaw god came to snatch him from fate's fond embrace.

His business took off. As he grew bolder, he raided more of the blue lights. As he grew richer, he expanded on the distribution side to other coastal communities and even inland. Before long he was supplying hundreds of people with drugs. He bought a villa on the Drive and a 68-foot Grebe motor yacht with two rescue boats hanging from davits near the stern, for easier raiding. Milo, his partner at first, lost his nerve after about six months, predicting a bad end to it all and taking the boat he'd procured in the first place with him, so Jack the Cat invested in the yacht.

Those were good days, long, languid, power-hungry days for Jack the Cat. He now understood just what was possible for a man with his celestial gifts. The time when talking to cops was like stabbing himself in the throat was gone, and he discovered a glib enough style to socialize with anybody—captains, sheriffs, mayors, state senators, real estate developers, pharmaceutical executives, you name it. He took to wearing power suits made of cashmere, eating out at East Brother restaurants he'd never even known were there in his former life, and driving around town in a silver Rolls Royce Corniche.

He discovered how much a natural he was at building empires. It was a calling, or an obsession. He didn't care about anything or anyone else. If you asked his old Del Mar Street friends, they'd say he was turning into a total asshole, but from his point of view that was just envy, and he was probably right. Jack the Cat was a mogul in the making, and only three things that he could see stood in his way.

Sometimes he still wondered where the drugs came from and who he was ripping off. This was a wild card in the system, one sign of benediction too obvious either to accept without some sort of religious conversion or ignore with completely cynical Jack the Cat élan. Most of the time he ignored it, but the question remained, haunting his schemes, aggravating a desire for more and more control over all aspects of the business. He'd started thinking of his empire as a complex glass machine that was visible only to him, and so only he could operate it. Of course, he saw the danger in this right away. Micromanaging could bring down even the most spidery multinational, if it got out of hand. Top-down authority was a relic from the good old days of state-organized capitalism. In an open economy you had to be a free spirit or you were dead. He tried to keep this in mind. He told himself he just wanted those transparent mechanisms and gears to run exactly as he commanded because they were beautiful. The appeal was artistic, not fascist—like sunlight in water, not Ahab on the Pequod. But he wasn't always sure he believed it.

The second thing impeding mogul-metamorphosis was a heroin habit he'd picked up along the way, unavoidable in his line of work. It snuck up on him pretty quickly, but since it dovetailed so well with all the fun he was having, he couldn't tell he had a problem for a long time. The urge toward pure voluptuousness was irresistible, even though it clouded his vision and blunted the sharp edges of his business mind. He sensed a catastrophe in the offing while he stewed deliciously in the hazy hot-tubs of the drug, soft mouths nibbling at the tips of his ambitions like foamy-haired nymphs, but he was unable to pull himself together. All he could do was juggle the two sides of his nature, mogul and sybarite, and pray to his supernatural benefactors that it would never come to a head.

The third thing was love and Hippolyta, whose possessiveness spiked in more or less exact proportion to Jack's success. In the East Brother he now inhabited, most girls were Amazons, and just about all of them would fuck him for one gram of cocaine. Not surprisingly, temptation came to be felt like the cravings of a desert saint. He tried his best to resist, but human willpower being what it is, lapses were just slightly less frequent than Hippolyta thought they were.

He looked long and hard for ways to improve his situation. He took more interest in cultivating his own sources in the drug-producing nations of the world, easing out of the dependence on stolen cargo. His first overtures were greeted with universal hospitality, and contacts grew so rapidly that he set sail one summer for the US Virgin Islands, seeking both a base of operations and escape from Hippolyta's webby clutches. His lawyers had arranged for all potential operatives to meet on St. Thomas the weekend of the summer solstice. Jack the Cat would be the event's host and keynote speaker.

Just outside the town of Charlotte Amalie there was an old stone fort built on three massive tiers. The upper tier, supporting a tower that jutted above crenelated embankments, housed the St. Thomas police department, under the direction of chief Carlos Calderon, a philosophical man who knew too much about the world to want more from it than good conversation, a bottle of mescal, and a cigar on the terrace of his office, with its capacious view toward St. Croix.

On the two lower tiers, dark, inward, and cellular, lived a throng of addicts, whores, Rastafarian anarchist pushers, hippies, survivalists, gurus and lamas who brought black market crime to new levels of spiritual accomplishment. Called Malparaiso, pirate capital of the Caribbean, it was the ideal place for Jack the Cat's felonious convention. Carlos agreed, after a little coaxing and a lot of old-fashioned bribery on that terrace.

It was a fun mix of people—Colombian growers from the highlands above Santa Marta, Cali cartel representatives, Oaxacan and Michoacán farmers, Jamaican pilots, gun runners with CIA contacts, Venezuelan agents provocateurs, ex-Green Berets turned mercenaries, bribable customs officials and airport security men, Tranquilandia chemists, Wo Hop To middlemen from Hong Kong, death squad commanders, and Peruvian revolutionaries. Festivities included makeshift stalls showcasing goods and parties with themes like "Psychoactive Effects of Kick-Ass Guatemalan Mescaline" or "Benzedrine and Methedrine: Contrast in Style or Substance?" Incidental tensions, a stabbing, one political squabble touching off a small riot, a mysterious case of food poisoning, marred the proceedings, but otherwise everyone was happy, and Jack the Cat steered it all to his final triumph, the ritual signing by torchlight of the contract that gave birth to the empire in its global form. A conduit was duly set up, running from various tributary points through the Virgin Islands to the willing consumers of East Brother, whose pockets were deep when it came to effective disorganization of the human mind.

Over time this system of flows grew more ornate. New sources were diverted into the central current from places as far away as Thailand and Morocco, a development that appealed to Jack the Cat's aforementioned taste for the exotic. East Brother had more variety of highs to choose from than anywhere in the southwestern United States. He had connoisseur crops of skunk weed from the Hindu Kush Range in Afghanistan, temple ball hash from Nepal, the best Indian ganja and the best Thai sticks. He had South African zol, so cerebral it could turn surfers into professors in a hot second. He had Malawi hemp, wrapped in bark and tightly rolled, two hits of which transformed the ordinary world into the Eye of God Nebula. He had the finest grade coca leaf the black dirt of Mesoamerica could produce, the best Vietnamese opium, the usual assortment of shatter, wax, acid, angel dust, uppers and downers. His empire spread out like the Nile, and the location of its fabled sources sparked growing fascination among casual user and junkie alike, who began to see in Jack the Cat a figure of almost mythic proportions. Legends sprang up, putting him in places as far-fetched as the Kremlin or Jupiter, where with the divine guidance of luminaries like Krishna, Dan Quayle, and Magic Johnson, he was busy negotiating for ever more bitchin' psychoactive substances.

The pressure of being mythic would have done any man in, and Jack the Cat, to his credit, handled it better than most. Drugs were his sole crutch, unfortunately, and before long his heroin habit had become a massive heroin habit coupled with a coke habit, and the combination, while producing ever finer degrees of euphoric transport, also made him moodier, more peevish, by turns personable and vicious, lucid and totally insane.

He finally dumped Hippolyta in one of his down-turns. She'd become such a harridan that even the small moments of relief he managed to find for himself were tarnished by her jealousy.

"What's your problem?" he said.

"Your dick, is what's my problem," she cracked. "And all those bitches you're sticking it in, that's what's my problem."

"We're rich. We're having fun, relaxing, hanging out—"

The only thing I see hanging out's between your legs."

"And I suppose you haven't been getting it on the sly your own self?"

A large crystalline ashtray sailed just above his head and banged loudly against the wall behind him.

"If I'm wrong, I'll cop to it," he said, running for cover behind a yellow Pedro Friedeberg hand chair, "but seems like I've been seeing Moley around a lot lately."

A barrage of household items turned projectiles hit the chair, and Jack the Cat felt the tremolo that typically prefigured a swoop of sudden violence. Hippolyta made the choice clear: either her, or the empire, and Jack the Cat did not, could not, hesitate.

"That's it," he said. "You're out of here, Hippolyta. I've had it. Alfred! Samson!"

From behind the bar, where they'd been riding out this latest fight, Jack the Cat's two Samoan bodyguards, both former All-American defensive linemen at USC, lumbered to his side.

"Throw the bitch out," he ordered. They paused long enough to assess the fighting power of their new adversary, who stood her ground, eyes smoldering, arms akimbo, on her brand-new Persian rug.

The struggle was awesome. Jack had never seen anybody fight the way Hippolyta did then. It was like *Attack of the Fifty Foot Woman*. Before Alfred and Samson could get proper holds on her, she'd trashed the whole living room, broke everything from a Ming Dynasty vase to the set of cobalt blue highball glasses she bought for $40,000 in Rio to the sliding glass door leading to the deck.

In the end, though, Alfred and Samson got Hippolyta's sinewy body in vise-like half-nelsons, and they carried her squirming like a huge pissed off eel down the driveway to the front gate. There a steely Jack the Cat told them to deposit her on the sidewalk, which they did without ceremony.

As the gate clanged shut again, Hippolyta, exhausted, her face flushed crimson, raised her fist at Jack the Cat standing in the driveway and made a maleficent prediction. She said:

"This ain't over, Jack. You'll see. I'll be back. Oh man, will I be back. And if you aren't dead first, I'm gonna make sure you feel just what it's like to be me out here now, I swear to fucking God. You watch. What goes around, comes around."

His life improved after that. Sex without fear of retaliation or for the life of the woman in question was never better. Orgies without guilt were a different experience altogether. The effect was as soothing as any drug, and Jack the Cat could, without too much trouble, ignore the quality of curse in Hippolyta's words.

Until, that is, rumor reached him that she'd shacked up with a Pakistani guy named Tariq. He'd gone to Oxford, spoke the King's English, wore smart Italian suits, and drove a 1964 Aston Martin. He had a reputation as a world-class traveler, a connoisseur of fine wines, and a hitman for the mob. Jack the Cat took the news with a smile on his face and pandemonium in his heart.

All out terror set in when word got around that Hippolyta had put a contract out on his life. He knew from experience that people like Tariq were not ordinary mortals, that they killed for a living not because the money's good or even because they liked it, but because they were naturals at their job, they had a talent just like Jack did, only it was for murdering people, not building empires. Nothing, he knew, not even Samoan bodyguards, could protect him from the divinely inspired. He was a dead man. He, Jack the Cat, in whose name cargo cults had sprung up, whose wealth was fabulous and whose lives had exceeded nine thousand, let alone nine—a dead man. He couldn't believe it. He spelled the words out for himself, and still he couldn't believe it. Death for Jack the Cat bore the grotesque masks of his paranoid theater, but never the dark-complected aspect of a suave Oxford-educated Pakistani assassin. Tariq was the kind of guy who took off the mask, left the stage, and started shooting at the gallery boxes where people like Jack the Cat were firing quarters behind the velvet curtains. He was an offense to the feeling, always so reliable, that death happened only to other people and that despite everything Jack the Cat would live forever.

This feeling most likely accounted for his eventual choice of hiding place. He considered all the remotest corners of the empire—the Himalayas, the Orinoco River, desert fjords on Baja, one or two little canyons tucked away behind Big Sur—but, in the end, he didn't even leave East Brother. He went to the place he figured no one in his circles would ever expect to find him: Milo's house on Josephine Street.

"What's wrong?" Milo wanted to know first off.

"Nothing, nothing," said Jack the Cat. "Come over to see how you were, that's all."

"No shit?" said Milo. "I don't see you for who knows how long, except in places like *Star* and *Covert Action*—"

"*Covert Action*?" cried Jack the Cat. "What am I doing there? What's a guy like me doing there?"

"You tell me."

"Don't do no business with the Feds or the CIA," muttered Jack the Cat, with a tired attempt at feeling.

"I don't want to know."

"No fucking way."

"I believe you."

"Listen, Milo...how's about I stay here for a few days, if it's all right with you?"

"Why?"

"Just a few days," he urged. "I need the time, you know, to get away from the limelight for a while."

Milo was suspicious.

"I swear, on...on the bible of the empire, that I'm not conning you. Do you know how much that's worth, for me to swear on the bible of the empire?"

"Come off it," said Milo. "You think I'm stupid? It means Jack the Cat's looking out for himself, same as it always has."

"I'm hurt, Milo," he said, "hurt that you think the word of the empire is cheap. My word, okay, fuck it, worthless." He spit on Milo's fir floor. "But the empire, Milo, the empire..." Its sanctity overwhelmed all speech.

Milo was just smart enough to know Jack the Cat was lying to him, but not worldly enough to guess why or that it boded more ill for him than anything ever had in his life. He assumed the usual reasons for hiding out, on the usual small scale, in spite of Jack the Cat's reputation, those bizarre stories about trips to Timbuktu and meetings with old Mongol kings, those fabulous rumors of buried treasure and sexual excess that he'd heard on the streets and wondered about many a lonely night.

"I s'pose it's okay," he said then sulkily.

Straight off Jack the Cat closed all blinds and locked all sashes and doors.

"What are you doing?"

"Thanks," said Jack the Cat, "thanks, I'm just…you know, tidying up, I always liked it dark here…on Josephine Street."

"Uh-huh."

"Good times, yeah, it'll be good times, just the two of us, you watch."

As he spoke, he took a black velvet blanket from the valise he had with him, crouched backward into the slot between Milo's sofa and the drafting table in his living room, and shrank into its folds until only the bridge of his nose was visible. Milo watched him with cold surprise.

"Fuck, man," he said at last.

"What?"

"Least you could do is bring some of that limelight down off the mountain when you come," he said, shaking his head.

For almost a month Jack the Cat lived in the space between sofa and table, getting up only to pee, shit, and shoot up. Milo could see the telltale signs of drug abuse, the tracks in his arms, the collapsed veins, the worn strung out look of a junkie. It confirmed Milo in his suspicion that East Brother had become a much tougher place than it used to be. Hustling wasn't the same anymore. People were pooling their talents, dealers were hiring middlemen and middlemen touters. You had to have information people just to know where the fences were. Gone were the days when a free agent like Milo could hang with it.

The two of them got along pretty well. Milo, rather than watch Jack the Cat starve, since eating hardly ever occurred to him, consented to make peanut butter sandwiches or sloppy joes for dinner. Sometimes, with Jack on a particularly mellow nod, they'd reminisce about the old days.

But Jack the Cat wouldn't tell him what kind of trouble he was in. The cryptic hints he did drop led Milo to think it had to do with his old lady Hippolyta, which made sense, so he chalked it up to old lady troubles and left it at that, until the month had gone by and Jack the Cat showed no signs of leaving. Then he started to think there might be more trouble than he imagined. It wasn't until the morning he saw the man with the suit turn into his driveway, though, that the full significance of his situation came home to him.

"There's a man with a suit in my driveway, Jack," he said, peering through the jalousie slats in his living room window.

"Holy fucking shit!"

Danger instantly communicated itself to Milo. He fell to the floor and crawled over to the sofa.

"What is it, Jack?"

"You got to answer the door," he hissed.

"Are you crazy?"

"No, no, you're right. Don't open the door. What am I thinking?"

"You know this guy?"

"Oh shit, oh shit, oh shit, oh shit."

"What does he want, Jack?"

"Oh shit, oh shit, oh shit, oh shit."

Milo went under the table and considered. It was clear the guy wanted to mess with Jack in some way, and if so, Milo was going to be a witness. Which meant the guy was also going to mess with Milo. When, at that point, he heard the knob on his front door rattle sharply, all presence of mind collapsed.

The knob rattled a second time. Then the whole door rattled. Then the panes in the window next to the door rattled. A progression of rattles went around the house to the side door and returned to the living room, where one last rattle diminished into silence. Both men held their breaths.

The sound of shattered glass set them both whimpering. A hand in a natty gabardine sleeve with gold cufflinks reached through the broken window to the top of the sash, fumbling with the lock. A moment later the sash went up with a bang and Tariq stepped into the room by pushing the blind forward. A heavy scent of Egyptian musk filled the air. With a crash the blind fell back against the sill, producing another round of whimpering from the floor.

"Come on out," said Tariq.

Neither moved.

"I'm not going to hurt you."

Neither heard.

"I'm just here to tell my man Jack why I'm not going to kill him."

"You're what?" said Milo.

"Come out of there!" he cried.

"He's not going to kill me," said Jack the Cat dazedly.

"He's not going to kill me," said Milo dazedly.

"I can't believe it," said Jack the Cat, even though he knew he could believe it, and always had believed it.

"I went to the Virgin Islands looking for you, did you know that?" said Tariq. "That's a long fucking distance to travel, just to tell somebody you're not going to kill him."

"It is," Jack the Cat agreed.

"I want you to remember that when I give you my reason."

"It's trepanned into my skull."

"The reason I'm not going to kill you," Tariq said, pausing for emphasis, "is money."

"Money?" said Jack the Cat.

"That's right. For this job I took ten thousand dollars from Hippolyta, which is a fraction of my usual take. Are you following?"

"I am."

"I figure by not killing you, I could expect many times that amount. Is that right? Tell me."

"That's right," said Jack the Cat, thinking Tariq might be a man he could work with. The math was blowing Milo's mind. Neither of them had managed to get off the floor.

"But even that's not what I want."

"It's not?"

"No," said Tariq. "I mean, it is what I want, but I want more, too."

"No problem," said Jack the Cat. "Money's no object."

"Money's not the point."

"You just said it was."

"Uh-uh," Tariq said, annoyed. "You're not following. I said I want more than money."

"You've got to be clear," said Jack the Cat, "when it's business."

"Absolutely."

Tariq made it clear. He wanted a job. He wanted to be Jack the Cat's exclusive hired assassin. It wasn't worth killing someone as capable of expanding horizons as an international drug mogul like him.

This unexpected turn of events had Jack rising from the floor into a still more turbocharged sense of possibility. He put his arm around Tariq's shoulder as they ambled through the front door, conniving in low whispers about their future partnership. He was so preoccupied he didn't even manage to say good-bye, which would have bothered Milo if his heart wasn't still pounding like a diesel hammer in his chest. All he could do was stand flat footed on his porch, watch the two of them disappear onto Josephine Street, and wonder what the hell the world was coming to.

Jack the Cat moved to the next level of imperial aspiration so naturally you'd have thought he was groomed for it from day one. In fact, a childhood spent on the Lower East Side of Manhattan did serve as a valuable initiation. He rediscovered the ghetto in penthouses, boardrooms, and Miami Beach mansions. All it seemed he had to do, in negotiations with other international gangsters, was think of long-lost friends and talk to them as though for the first time in years. He had no idea why this worked, and sometimes the things he said sounded like gibberish even to him. But it never mattered. People kept answering him back as though they knew what he was talking about, and the deals went through every time. It was, indeed, getting harder and harder to avoid the idea of a cosmic plan ordering Jack the Cat's magnificent life.

So much power accrued to him, finally, that even the biggest Forbes 400 CEOs began to take notice, inviting him to see their foremost public relations man in his Washington D.C. office. Jack showed up in top form. The walls curved, but only because they really did curve. Their dialogue was a marvel of miscommunication.

"Boots!" said the man, gazing at the sparkly specimens he wore propped on the desk in front of him. Jack the Cat could see only their silver-tipped toes over a clutter of family photographs, each turned outward for his guests to peruse. "Boots remind me of a story." Two watery eyes swam over the picture frames. A hand trailed limply to one side and back again. He wore a Stetson hat and seemed to suffer from a head cold. "My great granddad was the only hero to survive the butchery of the Alamo, did you know that?"

"My grandfather carved carousel horses for a company in the Bronx," said Jack the Cat. That was a lie. Jack the Cat's grandfather was an optician from Ljubljana, a doddering old polisher of lenses.

"Is that so?"

"It is. And I'll tell you another thing: he knew what he was doing."

"He did?"

"He was the best wood carver in America. Right up there with Looff."

"No!"

"Yes!"

They remained silent for a moment.

"I always loved the Looff carousels best," the man said.

"They're pretty bitchin'."

"They remind me of a story. My great granddad was shot in the back by Jesse James."

"That's rough."

"It is. You see, he stole a pair of boots that belonged to the outlaw, and since Jesse had such a discriminating sense of right and wrong, he killed my great granddad to serve as an example."

This was as close to pointed as either man ever got.

"Jesse James had a lot of balls," remarked Jack the Cat.

"He did. I wish he wouldn't've stolen all that money from the banks and given it to the poor, is all. That *was* unseemly."

Silence. Jack the Cat noticed sweat lightly precipitating on the man's jowly cheeks.

"Herbert Hoover is under-appreciated," he went on, "don't you think?"

"How's that?"

"Herbert Hoover."

"I don't have nothing to do with the Feds or the CIA," averred Jack the Cat. "That's just a code with me."

"I understand. I remember my days as a Texas youth, the prairie, the young Mexican girls from Matamoros—"

"They grow some good dope by Matamoros."

"They were," he assented. "But they liked to have sex, so we had a good time anyway."

"Stuff's got too many seeds in it to be first-rate locoweed, though."

The old man's brow shot up into a triangle, and a wave of annoyance passed through his runny eyes. He said:

"We don't need to be lewd, Mr...um...? What's your name again?"

"I've got a million of them. You can call me Jack."

"Jack. Jack? Jack Kennedy. Jack Ruby. Jacqueline Bisset. Jack Sprat. Jack Daniels. Jack Nicholson. Jack the Ripper. Jack-in-the-Pulpit. That reminds me of a story."

And around they went. Words seemed to evanesce as they were spoken, to hang in the air like the misty spray enveloping the old guy's head, Stetson hat and all. The only piece of information Jack the Cat hung on to was a date to meet somebody named "Roman Candle" at the Bohemian Grove, and by the time he flew back to East Brother to prepare for that, the halo of mist had thickened to a fog so dense he couldn't even be sure there'd been a meeting at all.

This was an inauspicious sign for the trip to the Bohemian Grove. Jack the Cat intended to limo up the coast and hobnob with the Bechtels, swim a little, frolic through the redwoods as powerful men had been doing up there for decades. His body, however, had another plan. It had been coming for a while now. Heroin has a way of doing that: creeping up from behind and thwacking you on the head when you least expect it. He'd been out of control for too long. He was nodding even when he wasn't nodding. The whole world turned in the ludic cycles of a perpetual high. A hundred times he'd taken a little too much, gone a little too far, and nothing happened. Limits dissolved before his eyes; it seemed they were there only to go beyond. His surprise was extreme, then, when he shot the beast as usual one afternoon, the day before heading for the Grove, and maybe the syringe slipped or maybe he shot hot, but after a few seconds he lost his balance, broke his jaw on the porcelain lip of a kitchen sink, and blacked out on the floor.

He couldn't remember anything about the blackness, except that it was total, like the bottom of a tarpit. It lasted just long enough for Samson to reach the bathroom, lift him up, and administer frenzied blows to his face and chest. Jack the Cat saw them as phosphene fairies in a void, beckoning him back to consciousness with a delicacy he'd never before thought possible.

The amazing thing was that he woke up in a hospital the next day the same old Jack the Cat, in all his brilliance and all his loves, his vanities, his sorrows, his impenitent greed, his secret emptiness. A pack of ice lay on his groin, a bandage covered his face, and an IV had been thrust into his forearm. A dull crawling pain infested his organs and limbs where they weren't numb. But here, too, his spirit expanded. Here, too, he took in extremes no one by rights should have been able to survive, and did not break.

The craving for dope also survived the ordeal, and as soon as they released him from the hospital he found, with Tariq's help, a clinic in the Swiss Alps, renowned as a refuge for strung out rock-n-roll stars and anemic European royalty. Once he arrived, the doctors gave him blood transfusions, and after recycling his system they put him on methadone. Exchanging two sublime habits for one mediocre substitute made little sense at the time, but as long as Jack the Cat was there, he stayed with the program. For five months he lived in seclusion on Tragic Magic Mountain (an in-patient joke), getting perspective and gathering strength for another spectacular come back. Tariq, steward of the empire in his absence, sent regular reports to keep him abreast of the business.

The slow pace up on the mountain made for some interference in Jack the Cat's radar, however, because he didn't notice how vague those reports were becoming, how filled with incidental detail and prolix accounts of insignificant events. He talked to Tariq regularly on the telephone without the slightest suspicion of duplicity on the other end. His English accent always sounded so reassuring to him.

Proof of what had indeed already taken place came when the chief clinic administrator informed Jack the Cat that he had to leave that very day.

"What do you mean?" he cried. "For months I can't go down to the chalet for a pack of cigarettes, and now I'm on my ass?"

The administrator waved a piece of paper in his face. "Payments canceled," it said, in underscored letters. Jack the Cat called Tariq on his satellite phone. He got the information recording of the Nancy Reagan Human Resources Foundation, a shell company he'd set up for a pipeline of Maghreb kef into East Brother. He called a dozen numbers, and they'd all been changed. When he reached somebody he knew, he asked what was going on. Even then he thought there must be some minor problem that explained it all, some legal hang-up—civil forfeiture of the empire, say, an overzealous attorney general stirring up trouble. Just bribe the right people and everything would be fine.

The guy he reached said, "How do I know you're Jack the Cat?"

"It's me, man, the Cat. Jack. You know my voice."

"It could be," the guy said, "but it could be a thousand other lowlife ball-scratching head cases I hear around here, too."

"One voice you aren't going to be hearing much of," promised Jack the Cat, "is yours, soon as I get back to the ranch, asshole."

He had enough cash stashed under his bed for a flight to Miami. Once there, he found out how completely his life had changed when the manager of the Sunshine State Bank, his financial institution of choice in Florida, unceremoniously threw him out the door. He went in search of his best Cuban operative, Eulalio Trafficante, a bear of a man with a voice like an angel, and he wouldn't see him. Even the waiters at the Cricket Club, who once lavished attention on him, peered into his face as though trying to place it. He'd figured out, finally, that Tariq had taken over, rigged the empire to respond to his signature, his voice control, his bank account numbers, his computer passwords, and let the in-place system of baffles and screens close around him naturally. Jack the Cat could see just how transparent his empire had become by his total inability to see any of it anywhere.

The only clue he ever found was a photograph in Vogue magazine. He noticed it at a newsstand in Palm

Beach one day, glancing over someone's shoulder. There, on the page, in garish color, he saw Tariq in a sharkskin suit, smiling for the camera. More horribly, his ex-wife Hippolyta was there on his arm, decked out in a snow leopard print dress with flounces, her expression taut with gratified desire. They held martini glasses and stood by a sign that said Main Street along with Pia Zadora, Bono, and a life-size Mickey Mouse. The caption read: "Five hundred celebrities flock to Disneyland for Michael Jackson's gala birthday party."

Shattered by this discovery, Jack the Cat went to the beach in a fugue of outrage and heartache. His only hope of getting his empire back, he decided, lay with the people who counted: the smugglers, the snakeheads, the stevedores, the ship crews, the safe house operators, the station chiefs, the document vendors, and all the people who revered him as a trickster god of controlled substances. He had to find out how much power he had in the trenches. Empires can be taken over in one swoop, but myths die hard. The hub, the main valve, was St. Thomas, so he rustled up the money for a passage on a freighter to Charlotte Amalie and headed south.

The old fort buzzed as it always did the day he arrived. Trade flowed through in epic volume, and the sight gladdened Jack the Cat as nothing had for months. He went in incognito at first, not wanting to cause a riot, and ranged the aisles like a king returned secretly from the wars. He had only enough money to sample a little hash, which he found first-rate, just as it should be. The rich code of the marketplace–one finger for reefer, two for bam, three for 'caine–was like music of the spheres to him. He talked up a young man selling car stereos and found out Jack the Cat was more mythical than ever, in fact too mythical.

"Word is the Cat bought it in an avalanche on Magic Mountain," said the kid. "I don't believe it, though."

"Why not?"

"How can a dude die who wasn't ever born, you know? No one capable of holding a conversation with a Venusian, you hear me, could be, like, human, right? I mean, if I'm wrong I'll cop to it, but the Cat always seemed larger than life to me, somehow."

"What if I told you I was Jack the Cat?"

"I'd say you needed a shrink, dude. Nobody can be Jack the Cat."

"But look," he said, taking a T-shirt with his likeness on it from the next stall over. "See how much I look like him." He slipped the hood he wore from around his head and held the shirt up for comparison. "What would you say then, if I looked just like Jack the Cat?"

"I'd send you to my buddy Archie," the kid said, "'cuz he looks just like the Cat himself. Man, the Cat's an archetype, understand? He's everywhere. They've been having Jack the Cat lookalike contests in Malparaiso for years."

The kid gave Jack the Cat a doubtful look, not sure whether he should be talking to a guy who didn't know that. He moved a few feet down the aisle on which he was hawking his wares and started whispering to his neighbor, the T-shirt salesman.

Jack the Cat, in a panic, announced to everybody he met that he was Jack the Cat. Those who bothered to listen only laughed at him. Days and then weeks went by with him looking for believers. He found them everywhere, and none of them believed him. His life became a crusade at this point. He stood on buckets and proclaimed his identity. He sermonized by swimming pools and outside nightclubs. He hung around the yacht harbors in the hope of spreading the word to other islands in the archipelago. He made posters, wrote a pamphlet telling his story, logged long hours preaching to fellow indigents, and started writing "Jack the Cat was here" on the walls with stolen spray paint cans.

So much tireless dedication sucked in his cheeks, hollowed out the wells of his eyes, and stretched his leathery skin taut. His unkempt hair congealed into a single rug-like shag around his shoulders, and his feet became calloused stumps. His voice went permanently hoarse from so much oratory. When his bony hand shot out at you from within the folds of his dirty rags, it was like an eel ambushing prey. He did that a lot in front of the major hotels and at the airport, since it was usually good for a dollar or two, if nothing else.

The situation of being and not being Jack the Cat wore him down after about ten years. He no longer knew what was true. It had him wondering if his memories weren't only the after-effects of a very bad trip. That's what Carlos Calderon thought. They'd been on good terms from the time of the convention right up to the day Jack the Cat died in a single-engine Cessna when it went down over the Sargasso Sea. He liked to ease his friend's burdens when he could with bits of homespun metaphysical wisdom.

"In this day and age, compañero," he said over navy sours at the Bar Picard on Eisenhower Avenue, "we take what we can get as it comes and don't ask too many questions."

"Easy for you to say."

"What is existence, anyway?" Carlos inquired. "This... thing we call being alive. Eh? What do you or I understand about it? Molecules teeming in the brain. What can that mean? We are hopeless, let's face it, compañero, and time arches over us like a wave to pass us by. Isn't it better to say that all life is, is phenomena escaping us? That life, in its very nature, is to escape from knowing?"

"I don't want to know what life is. I just want to know why I'm always thinking I'm Jack the Cat."

"You are Jack the Cat," said Carlos.

"And you're Jack the Cat, and this table's Jack the Cat, and the fucking brass buckle on your belt is Jack the Cat," said Jack the Cat vehemently.

"That's not exactly what I meant."

"It's all relative, man, this stupid island voodoo Jack the Cat rip-off crap. It don't help at all with the fact that

I can't sleep nights remembering things like how you and me used to kick it on my yacht, talking about the empire and drinking piña coladas by moonlight."

"Those were fine times."

"See! You're fucking with my head. This whole place's conspiring to drive me crazy."

"What is 'crazy'?" mused his friend. "How do you define it?"

"I'm crazy! You're crazy! We're all crazy!!! I ain't gonna talk to you no more," Jack said, and sipped his navy sour in sullen silence.

"Maybe," ventured Carlos after a beat, "it's time for you to make a change. Maybe you need to face your demons."

"Nobody faces nothing in this place."

"So leave, compañero. Go home."

That sparked the idea of returning to East Brother and abandoning the cause altogether. With it came a new sobriety. He cleaned himself up, exchanged the rags of the saint for the rags of a salesman criminal, and began squirreling money away for the trip. In his opinion it would lead to the usual dead ends, but that was all right. By the time he set sail for Panama he didn't care anymore who Jack the Cat was. The whole question bored him.

He wandered up the isthmus from Colon, staying out of people's way, trying not to get into trouble. Except for a close call with a mugger near the canal, it was smooth sailing till he hit a Choco village on the west coast, where he was singled out for attack by a flock of scarlet macaws. They spied him in a crowd of American tourists like he was some kind of ideal food or nest-building material, and drove him one hundred yards into the shelter of a portable toilet, where they kept him under siege till nightfall. At the Costa Rica-Nicaragua border town of La Penca, he narrowly escaped dismemberment when a bomb went off. He wandered into the midst of an assassination attempt conducted by the military on a peasant activist in Honduras and only extricated himself with the help of the Honduran commander's chief adviser, who hailed from San Clemente, California.

After stumbling on a military drill in El Salvador and a village raid by civil patrols in Guatemala, Jack the Cat made it to Mexico. A revolution in the La Realidad forest of Chiapas made for slow-going, what with road checks every couple of miles and a lot of belligerent soldiers running around, but at last he reached the Oaxacan border. From there he zig-zagged through cannabis country before hitting the coast by Acapulco.

He decided to stay awhile in a place called Nahual. He lived in a garret above the shop of an old woman who made dolls with detachable stomachs. Inside them she put other smaller dolls you could take out and put in again. She made them from ceramic molds, painting the stuccoed faces red and yellow.

For some reason she thought Jack the Cat was a riot. She laughed at everything he did, whether or not it was funny. She liked the bird mannerisms best, and it got to the point where the second he turned up, she put her dolls down to impersonate him. She cocked her head, curled her wrists and bent fingers into talons, and stared at him with blank, reptilian eyes.

"Stop that!" he said on the day it started to piss him off. "I ain't no quetzal bird, so leave me alone."

She lowered her head beneath an upraised arm and nibbled fussily at her flight feathers.

"Stop that!" he said again. "Don't you got anything better to do than pester innocent bystanders like me?"

"Forgive me, senor," she sputtered hilariously. "I only observe the obvious."

"What?"

"That you are turning into a bird."

"I am not!" he cried. "I've just always been like this. It's just the way I am."

"Of course, of course, senor," she said, preening her wing.

A landlady who copied everything you did could drive even the sanest person insane, let alone Jack the Cat, so before too long he left again, hooking up with a migrant convoy headed for El Norte. From Tacámbaro it took him down into the hotlands of Michoacán, stopping at ranchos to pick up more emigrados, and it rolled into Guadalajara about two days later. The further he went, the easier he felt. A few quick changes pulled on gas-station attendants and some three-disc monte in

Mazatlán really got his juices flowing. After that it felt as if the dream was his sojourn in the Virgin Islands, and his journey back the way to some new awakening.

In Tijuana he got hold of a beat-up, bullet-ridden Mercury Grand Marquis and lived out of that for a while. By selling as cocaine bags of procaine mixed with flour to green Navy seamen, he raised enough to pay a coyote to drive the car across the border. Since Jack the Cat was a blank in just about every data base in America, he had to sneak across with a group of illegals by crawling for miles through an abandoned sewer pipe.

Once in San Diego he got the Mercury back and headed for East Brother. He went to the villa straight off. It was still there, though locked up and in apparent disuse. An old retiree on the Drive told him every now and then a helicopter flew in and flew out again, but mostly it stood empty. Jack the Cat looked forlornly through the wrought-iron gate and wondered how his two Samoan bodyguards were doing, if they were his two Samoan bodyguards. He climbed the wall and broke in through a window. He found an old familiar bed, but the kitchen cabinets were bare and the hot tub was drained and choked with leaves. The thought of crashing there was almost too much to bear, but he stayed anyway, at least until something better came along.

No one on the streets believed he was Jack the Cat, of course, and no one wanted to do business with a stranger who said he was Jack the Cat either. He had such a hard time hustling that he hired himself on at the Donat Brothers Glass Company as assistant to the master glass-makers. It was his first real job since he stocked liquor at the Lucky Dog on Delancey Street when he was twelve.

Depression weighed on him, but he found his powers of resistance grew as he settled into an ordinary beach town life, letting the littoral days carry him along. A healthy bloom returned to his face, and people came to know him by his quick-winged, hummingbird-like idiosyncrasies.

One feathery summer day, about six months after his return, he was tacking through town for no particular reason, just to see what he could see, and thought of his friend Milo. He banked up Escondido Avenue to Josephine Street and knocked. To his surprise he saw this old guy he didn't recognize.

"Sorry," he buzzed. "Wrong place. Thought somebody I used to know lived here."

He backed off from the porch, turning around as he went, and would've flown off if the old guy hadn't said, "I can't believe it."

Jack the Cat hovered.

"What can't you believe?"

"Jack the fucking Cat. I thought you'd died."

"Yeah?"

"They said a Bengal tiger had you for lunch in Sri Lanka."

"Well, I guess I'm not dead."

"Hell no, you look as crazy as ever."

"You really think it's me?"

"Of course it's you," said Milo.

"Yeah, right. Of course. I don't remember you being so old," he said, heading inside.

Milo wasn't so old. He had, though, been in retreat from a world that had long since stopped making sense to him. These days he hardly left his house except for cigarettes, food, and money when he could eke some out.

"You're not a salesman no more?" asked Jack the Cat. "No more mixing it up with the lowlife crowd?" He sounded disappointed.

"Been out a long time, Jack. It seemed like everything got strange, or I got strange, and things could go on without me pretty well."

"I'm straight, too, I guess."

"No more empire, huh?"

"I have plans."

"I guess you know you can leave me out."

"I have this lamp company."

"Uh-huh."

"I mean, I work for this lamp company, and they make this glass in these huge burners. There's four of them in the factory, right, and they keep them lit all the time, because it takes weeks to get them up to temperature. They look like Cheshire cats, all of them."

Milo's face fell.

"Now I got me this key—"

"They gave you a key to the whole place!"

"Yeah, and there's all this scrap glass, you know, cullet and batch shit, lying around—"

"Respectable businessmen gave you a key to their shop!"

"Yeah."

"The most untrustworthy cat in all of East Brother and probably the world, and they lay it open for you to plunder!"

"I'm not going to rip them off," said Jack. "The stuff I'm talking about is scrap, junk, garbage."

"How come you're so lucky?" demanded Milo. "That's what I want to know. How come everything just sort of falls into your lap?"

"I don't know, Milo."

"I hate this world, I hate it. And you know what? It's you that makes me hate it. I hate it because, in it, guys like you always end up coming out ahead, while I sit here like a one-eyed cat peeping in the seafood store."

"Do you want to hear about my glass or not?"

"Fuck the glass! I'm talking about cosmic evil and you're talking about glass. What's the matter with you?"

"I suppose I'm crazy, Milo."

"That's right. Because anybody who wants to talk about glass in a world this set up against decent, ordinary people has got to be crazy."

Milo snapped on his little color television. The tinny sound of small striving voices welled into the kitchen.

He turned the channel, and Jack the Cat heard the bland tones of a newscaster's voice.

"See!" said Milo, pointing at the screen. "A refinery accident! A cloud of poison's released into the air and the wind blows it right over the poor neighborhoods, missing the fancy suburbs.

"Or here, here," he said, picking up a newspaper from the table. "Listen to this: 'More people were killed in weekend car accidents over the last ten years than died in the Vietnam and Iraq wars combined.' Combined!"

Milo flung the paper down and started channel surfing.

"Something's wrong," he went on. "I can't put my finger on it, but something's definitely wrong. Look!" He pointed at the TV again. "Boat people. Boat people from Africa trying to sneak in to Greece. Human cargo. Refugees sailing hundreds of miles on rubber dinghies, and for what? So they can live like church mice paying their smugglers back, that's what."

The two men sat around the table and watched a litany of disasters flash across the screen. Jack the Cat had to admit things looked pretty bleak. Earthquakes, droughts, tsunamis, typhoons, terrorism, civil wars, failed states—one thing going wrong after another. That's all the TV seemed to do: report on what went wrong.

But what did that matter, Jack the Cat thought, when there was this colored glass lying around like gravel at the glass factory?

They made glass for Tiffany lamps, the kind with swirls in it. Jack the Cat didn't see the opportunity right away. He stared at the mounds of glass he tended on a daily basis, thinking of other things, the past, the glory days, but one afternoon, carting another load from the slumped glass department to the dump in back, it suddenly occurred to him that he was carting another load from the slumped glass department to the dump in back.

On his next day off he gathered some of the cullet into boxes. He found a fifty-five-gallon drum at the dump and set up his own tumbler next to the derelict hot tub at the villa. Mixing in sand, he rolled the glass till it came out polished. Then he took the pieces to the gift shops in East Brother, and straight off the salesmen started retailing them for three dollars apiece. Before Jack the Cat knew it he was bringing in two hundred dollars a week. He started a business: Glass Is a Gas Collectibles, Ltd., Jack Wind, Proprietor.

Milo couldn't believe it. He went with Jack one day to the glass factory, to see for himself what he had going, and damn if there wasn't enough leftover glass to furnish an empire with little glass collectibles.

"And they just let you take it?" he said.

"Man, they pay me fifty bucks a ton to get rid of it. Although, Milo," he added, his voice sinking like a stone in water, "they don't know I'm getting as big a dividend as I am, so don't be talking."

"No one talks to me," declared Milo, "and I don't talk to anybody, so you don't have to worry."

"You old misanthrope," said Jack the Cat affably, ducking back into the Mercury Grand Marquis parked out front. They headed down to Del Mar Street, Milo nervous at a beer Jack the Cat sipped casually as he drove. Such disregard for the fascist urge-to-bust-ass in every East Brother police officer Milo had ever known made the sapling of his nature quake sensitively. When they pulled over on Del Mar and Jack the Cat dropped a plump joint that rolled to the foot of a street ventriloquist talking up a Charlie McCarthy doll, Milo's heart bent clear down to the ground.

"That looks like some good times," drawled the ventriloquist's doll, as the ventriloquist picked up the joint and handed it back.

"Shut up, asshole," said the ventriloquist.

"Shut up the two of you," said Milo, looking both ways along the street. "They'll send us to Tehachapi soon as they see reefer. Watch it."

But Jack the Cat's irrepressible indifference to laws got the better of his careful nature that day. To Milo's stupefaction, the three of them, Jack the Cat, the ventriloquist, and the ventriloquist's doll, huddled down an alleyway a half-dozen feet or so and got high. Milo couldn't carry a grocery bag down Del Mar Street without getting hassled, yet here they were toking in broad daylight and no cop in sight.

Jack the Cat's business took off in the months that followed, and the only hint of his mortality Milo could see—aside from the fact that he'd quietly started using heroin again—was a bunched up newspaper Jack the Cat kept in the inside pocket of his jacket, to simulate a handgun. Too much was at stake, he said, poking obsessively at the veins in his arm, not to be a total professional about it.

He decided to take a business trip to LA, since he heard about this guy there who rolled the glass in two-hundred-gallon drums. For a modest price he could polish more and bigger pieces of glass than ever before. His inventory thus enlarged, he took the tumbled glass to trade shows and gift shops, tirelessly touting their commercial appeal. He talked to anyone who'd listen about the future of glass. He sold them to Russian émigrés at the palisades in Santa Monica, movie stars at Laker games, roller bladers on Venice Beach, Mexicans who sold fruit under rainbow-colored parasols on street corners. He even went door to door on the off chance someone would buy them. That seemed to Milo, later, like a waste of time, except it's how Jack the Cat met the president of Aquariums, Incorporated at his home in Bel Air, and came away with a lucrative contract to make glass ornaments for fish tanks.

And not long after that, setting up a display case at a fleamarket in Anaheim, he met a tall, willowy woman with flowing red hair and freckled skin, named Moira Artemisia, MA, MFCCI, CHT, M.R.C.S., L.R.C.P., N.D.,

C.M.T., I.C.A.S. (she showed him her cards), a multi-dimensional spiritual counselor, clairvoyant, mandala weaver, chakra journeyer, cowrie-shell diviner, aromatherapist, and channel healer. She had this idea that his glass could pass for crystals in the burgeoning field of New Age crystallomancy, sort of a shamanistic-astrological-psychotherapeutic method much in demand by everyone from downsized defense industry employees to hotshot software engineers on the lookout for personal growth. She added that, as an Expert Intuitive and first-rate Zentrepreneur, she should be able to arrange any and all promotional opportunities he might require. The possibilities, she said, darting amorous glances his way, were pretty much endless. Jack the Cat, taking this in from somewhere well beyond amazement, had no reason to think she was wrong.

4

The Glass House

Later that evening Jack the Cat lies sleeping on the faux suede couch in Milo's living room, his Panama hat drawn down over his eyes and shading the dark O of his open mouth. As soon as he'd finished telling his story an irresistible weariness descended on him, and he could hardly make it to the couch before passing out. Milo says he falls asleep all of a sudden like that a lot. It has to do with the methadone, the fact his liver's shot, and who knows what else is wrong with him after all those years in the fast lane.

He sits with Jess on the carpet, both of them fiddling with old stereopticons and musing on the many paradoxes of Jack's life. Milo warns his nephew not to believe the half of it. No one is better than Jack at playing fast and loose with the truth. But even Milo has to admit some things did sort of happen the way Jack said, including the hitman—although the after shave he wore wasn't musk but patchouli, he feels sure about that.

The world really does seem made for people like Jack, people who don't think twice about what they're doing. People with a lot of drive. Milo likes hanging around with them, but in his heart of hearts he knows he's a lesser star in their galaxy, an ordinary person. He can't exactly say he'd rather be Jack. For one thing he wouldn't last a day at that metabolic rate. He's too ponderous. But even were it possible he'd have his reservations. As much as he might admire someone who throws himself into the mix like that, he can't help feeling there's a problem with it, too, something missed in bravado, even if it's just Milo peeping in the seafood store.

He's not as much of a grouchy stay-at-home as Jack seems to think, but it's true he's been more or less of the persuasion that the world's been walking into the marble orchard for a long time now. The only thing to do about it has been to watch from the sidelines, shore up what remnants of common sense he could still find, and never, ever forget that the emperor has no clothes. Mostly he's explained this to himself as not selling out. In the old days it was easy to do, since everybody pretty much had the same idea in mind. It was the Sixties, or thereabouts. The woods were Norwegian, the stones rolling, and the basements had medicine in them. It was hippies versus bikers, marijuana versus wine and reds, light shows, polka dotted T-shirts, Day-Glo, and rock bands at the Ace of Hearts down on Del Mar.

But all the excitement of that time has gone up the waterspout now, and Milo's lost confidence in the powers of understanding and change that run deep in his marginal life. He doesn't know where he stands anymore, or if there is even any place to stand. That margin has become a surface, and it flattens out a little more each day, robbing him of a vital third dimension. That's what the bitchin' guys like Jack miss—not just selling out, or even that they are selling out, but the consequences for everyone when there is nothing but selling out.

It bothers him that Jess might think less of him just because he's not a bitchin' guy. He wants to be an example for his nephew, somebody he can look up to, in part because Jess hasn't had many people like that around him. Certainly not his fat-ass dad, working every day at the escrow company. The only thing he's good for is a beer and a bowling shirt. His sister could sure pick them, man. Pat Cooper was the least dynamic guy you could imagine back in the day. All he'd ever known was tract-house living and trips to the mall, which left him dense about everything and happy to be it—not like Lucille, who grew up as Milo did in the Santa Ana Canyon and kept her bearings in a natural world of old crumbling barns, horsehair snares for catching rabbits, and cedar logs burning in the wood stove. It was a black day for Milo when they got married, because he knew she was turning against all that, opting for the modern world. But he didn't say anything. How could he? If Lucille got what she wanted, that means she got what she deserved, too. There wasn't anything more to say.

Jess, however, didn't deserve what his mom wanted. He'd always been a good kid, a sweet, rudderless kid lost on the sea of what his parents didn't know about themselves. He could use a little direction there. Maybe he could use a lot. Milo supposes he's giving it in his fashion. He wishes, though, that he had more to offer than baffled retreat.

But he tries not to let it worry him. Jess is going to think about him what he's going to think, and there's not a whole lot he can do about it. He is what he is: Milo Manning, the guy who lives in an old rotting landmark house and wanders around counting angels on the head of a pin. So what? There's a lot that's honorable in that. Why would his nephew think any less of him, just because he's not a legend?

Light in the living room is diffused, warm, thinning to shadows in the corners. Around them, on the plaster walls, foxed and yellow from years of accumulating smoke, hang old pictures in ornate gilded frames. These include a water color of a farmhouse nestled into the slip of a snow-covered valley, a lithograph of a man fishing from a canoe on a marshy lake, and an oil painting Milo did of a wind-contorted juniper in the Anza-Borrego desert. In spots where the frames have been taken down, rectangular white patches remain stenciled in on the walls. Aside from the sofa, there's also the drafting table scattered with brushes, squeezed tubes of paint, an airbrush with valve, an exacto knife, a harmonica, and torn off wings of Monarch butterflies that Milo's been trying to get right for one of his medallions.

He's taken out the box of stuff that belonged to his grandmother Lucy. It includes a cache of plates to be inserted in the stereopticon's mount. You hold it up by the wooden handle and slide the mount to find that exact point where the eye can't keep the twinned images on the plate distinct anymore and they blend into one 3-D illusion. Jess is deep now in the Constantinople of 1875. He has a bird's eye view of the city as it sweeps down hillsides to the Bosphorus. The detail is impressive. He can see loggias in distant houses with people standing on them, the minarets of mosques, narrow crooked streets, wharves with stevedores unloading cargo from tall ships. Boats dot the water—steamers, junks, and sampans. The biggest is a clipper ship. He can make out tiny sailors aloft in its rigging.

"I'm not much of an adventurer," he hears Milo say. "I always liked reading about adventures, but somehow I never wanted to be in one. I'm an avoider. If I can avoid terror, I do. I don't like terror. I've never gone in for bungee-jumping, hang gliding, or riding in airplanes ten feet off the ground and upside down. None of that Admiral Peary North Pole shit. I don't even like the rides on the boardwalk."

Jess feels the same, even if he has craved adventure. It was a reason for going into the Navy, beyond the aimlessness he hoped it would dispel. Adventure, though, is about the last thing he's found there. Mostly it's been as exciting as that midwatch on the fantail in low visibility fog, or staring for hours at snow on a monitor in a room the size of a closet, reporting every fifteen minutes into a microphone, "No contacts on sonar!" Even the travel hasn't been what it's cracked up to be. He's seen the same streets, industrial zones, and raggedy types of people in Honolulu, Okinawa, Manila, Brisbane—smelled the same smells, ate the same food, had the same conversations in the same bars with the same Navy seamen. The monotony of it all has been enough to jar the soul. The only thing he's been able to do really is shut down in the face of it, and he was too good at that already. He was there to break out of that, to be less introverted, less of an avoider. It's had him wondering if there is any breaking out of it. The more he tries, the more stuck in himself he gets.

Milo reaches over and slips an old cassette tape of Van Morrison's *Avalon Sunset* into a dusty stereo, and the soulful duet with Cliff Richards comes on. Jess mounts another plate, this one of a French cuirassier on a horse. He wears a three-cornered hat with a white feather in it, pulled down over one ear, and a sword in a scabbard hangs by his side. Behind him are the bivouacked tents of a regiment on a flat field that stretches toward a row of poplars. Jess sees dark figures in between the tents. He'd have been one of them if he were French then. Not an avoider but a lurker. A shadow. A ghost. He remembers a night coming off a ladderwell on his ship a few months' back. It was pitch dark except for red lights from the bow and a green light on the pier where they were docked. He'd just finished a watch and had a cigarette in his hand, green-colored in the red light, when he passed another seaman so caught up in what he was doing that he didn't even see him. And right then Jess felt like he wasn't there—like he was, in fact, a ghost, no more solid than that, haunting this place where men gave themselves over to rope and scrimshawed metal, bulkheads and machinery. It wasn't just a manner of speaking either. The feeling was real—not a different state but a purer state of his presence there, one he couldn't normally put into words. He was less a ghost on a sailing ship than a sailor on a ghost ship.

"You ever have anybody look at you like you were invisible?" Milo asks.

Jess smiles. "I was just thinking that."

"It's like they can't see you. They're looking at you, but they look right through you, too."

"Officers look at you that way, unless they want something or you've fucked up."

"My neighbors look at me that way," Milo tells him. "Like I don't exist, or they wish I didn't. I'm the pariah on the block: the only one without a remote garage door opener, an SUV, or a Guatemalan maid."

He recalls the years spent watching East Brother change into a town where he didn't belong. He took it personally, as if the Internet entrepreneurs and venture capitalists who started buying up all the houses were decamping in his kitchen. They might as well have been. It was personal. They didn't just live, they encroached.

They crowded you out. The guy next door is a case in point—tearing down a perfectly decent house and building his summer mansion right up to the property line, so Milo can feel like he's living next to Jonah's whale for the rest of his fucking life. What bothers him in that, more than the self-assertion, more even than the sense of entitlement, is the indifference, the carelessness toward others. All his neighbors show it, even the nicer ones. He knows this lady, for instance, who lives two blocks away. Her husband had been a colonel in the Air Force before he died in a plane crash ten years ago. Ever since she's been living off a military pension and working as the head librarian at the local branch. She's very liberal, helps with the homeless garden behind St. Brigid's Church, and organizes rallies for refugees and cancer victims. But when Milo really needed it, when he was really poor and nothing was working out for him, he tried to sell her some of his paintings, and she wouldn't buy a single one, not even knowing at some level that he was begging her for help. Sympathy went out the window. She looked right through him, like he didn't exist.

Jess loads up a picnic at Yosemite in the year 1897. He looks down a long table between two rows of diners to a man with a handlebar mustache and funny conical hat. Nobody seems very happy. They might have come from church or something. They're dressed in formal clothes, the men in suits and the women in bulky dresses and bonnets. He can see the plates and cups and silverware on the tables, along with two pairs of hands conspicuously interlaced in the foreground. They're in some kind of clearing, surrounded by redwood trees and charred stumps with opened tin cans placed on them. All the people at the table are perfectly in focus, but around them are the blurred bodies of children in motion. That's the only hint of frivolity. The stereopticon brings the whole scene into spectral relief.

"These things are incredible," he remarks. "You feel like you're right there in the 19<sup>th</sup> century."

"I wish I was there," Milo grumbles. "That's the time for me. I'd love to've been around before they had airplanes and cars and movie theaters and suburbs. Fuck the modern world."

Jess isn't so sure he agrees. He doesn't particularly like the modern world, but it doesn't seem all that great back then either. The stereopticon is working too well. It transports him into the past, but the past also loses some of its glamor. He can feel the weight of the present at that picnic table in Yosemite. Just like today, people in those days had to worry about what to do with themselves and what their futures would hold. They had to work jobs and live by rules and accept the consequences when they broke them.

He can't bring himself to consider just what that means for him now, beyond the stab of fear it produces. Instead he listens as Milo goes off on a tirade about suburbs and how timeless they are and how different it was even when he was growing up. "Orange County was all orchards back then," he says. "To go to Garden Grove you had to, guess what? drive for a long time through orange groves. We used to go over to Anaheim and Placentia just because it was scenic." They both laugh at that. "But then you started hearing about farmers selling off their land to build freeways and shopping centers. I remember watching them raze the orchards down with bulldozers. They left these huge piles of orange trees and made bonfires out of them. I'll never forget that. It was the eeriest thing I think I'd ever seen. Those fires could have been burning on Mars for all anybody could tell."

A wave of nostalgia, impossible to resist, carries Milo back to those vanished orange groves. They were magical places. He remembers the wind machines with their big propellers set up on stands, that the farmers used to keep air circulating. He remembers the spray sheds full of the pipes and hoses and nozzles they used to spray fish oil in the trees; that kept the oranges from freezing. And he remembers the standing pipes, about shoulder high, filled with water from underground aquifers, to irrigate with. People were always warning him not to go near them, since they were perfect traps for kids with acid on their mouths. Every so often one would drown. But he'd climb up anyway to get a drink of that clear cold water.

He goes into the kitchen and brings back some oranges. "Catch," he says, throwing one Jess's way. "Valencias." He peels one of his own and holds a peel up to his lighter. "Watch this." He flicks it on and squeezes. The flame flares out.

"It's the acid," he explains. "That's what's flammable. The peel itself doesn't burn at all."

They sit for a while, eating oranges and taking turns with the lighter. Spent peels accumulate on the carpet.

"I love fire," Milo says dreamily. "It's like a drug. I've started every fire I've had the chance to start my whole life."

That reminds him of his brown bag of marijuana. He goes in to the other room for it, too, and they proceed to smoke a few bowls.

"Lemme tell you," Milo says, on sucking in a hit, "I don't know what schizophrenic types like me would do without pot. I'm not a full-on schizoid, mind you, with visions and hearing voices and shit, but, well, my thoughts tend to wander in too many directions. I can't zero in on one thing at a time. When I'm working on a carpentry project, I start thinking about this painting project, and when I'm working on the painting project, I have this itch to go body surfing." They both lay flat on their backs and stare up at the ceiling. "I just can't be happy where I'm at. That's why I don't finish what I start."

"You finished those pictures in there."

"That's true. It wasn't easy though. Most days I woke up dreading it." Milo believes in work, and tedium is a part of work so he supposes he must believe in that, too. But there can be too much tedium, so much that it drives everything else out. "Don't get me wrong," he adds. "I'm not saying work should be a ride on the merry-go-round—even when you're working on a merry-go-round! But it should also give you what you need to feel happy in it."

"What do you need?"

Milo weighs his answer. "In my book happiness can't just be escape or fantasy," he says finally. "There have to be...reasons, I guess, behind the fantasies, which draw them out, which make them okay." This doesn't sound quite right. He takes another tack. "Say you're making a boat, and you're planing the wood for the planks, and you're making these nice round curls as you plane. That's a great feeling. That's what you need out of work—all you need for it to give you a sense of peace. Of course, there'll be times when it doesn't come out that way, and the curl you plane is cracked and brittle and falls to the ground. But that's okay. That's the gamble that keeps you honest."

"You have to zone into it," Jess offers, "so it becomes a dream."

"Kinda." Milo's not sure he likes the sound of that either. "You gotta be a wood cutter," he says, taking still another tack. "You work in the morning when it's sunny, then, when it rains, you keep right on going till it clears up again. You don't even notice that it's rained. You just keep right on cutting that wood, through pain, through adversity. That's what I mean by the 'dream.'"

Jess can't picture himself as this wood cutter. He knows what it's like to go on automatic while he works, but he's not sure it's ever more than a mechanism for getting through. Work for him means hearing the bosun on his ship wake everybody up with his bullhorn. "Reveille! Reveille! Reveille!" he cries. "All hands on deck. Sweepers fore and aft. Reveille! Reveille! Reveille!" Those words ring so desolately in Jess's ear he wants to melt away, to seep into his rack like a dinosaur into coal-tar. He doesn't, of course. He drags himself out to dress in the cold the same as everybody else, making his bed so smooth the petty officer can bounce a quarter off the sheet, and pretty soon he's swabbing that deck. But if the result is he feels less desolate, it's not because the dread is gone. It's still there, or always there...like a fact of life, a weight of the present.

Milo hardly ever gets the satisfaction he's talking about either. He thinks of all the dreary jobs he's had over the years—construction worker, tilesetter, drywall hanger, security guard, house painter. None has ever let him dream his way through pain and adversity. They're not even supposed to help with that. The point, if anything, is to separate the dream from the work, to cut it off from any reasons or need that would make both connect to something larger—a community, say, or a place, even a time. All that's left is each in isolation from the other, bad dreams and bad work for people in timeless suburbs. And the worst part is no one has much of a choice about it, once the split happens. The best anyone can do, it seems, is to help make the bad dreams a little better.

"Have I ever showed you Lucy's diary?" he asks, craving contact with the deeper world, the gone world.

"No." He has, once or twice, but Jess doesn't mind looking at it again. Lucy's his great grandmother after all. It's a wonder he even knows who that is.

Milo takes the leather-bound book from its shoebox, undoes its two metal clasps, and opens it. The diary spans the years before Lucy marries Edwin Kreel. The entries are brief and spare, written in neat print on pages formatted like a datebook, with chromolithographic arcs and foils on the edges. They start in Normal, Illinois, when she's sixteen and an orphan. Things look pretty bleak, Milo says. It's winter time, her parents die, then her sister dies, then a brother disappears. To make a living she has to work as a maid.

"'January 10, 1913, a drizzly day,'" he reads. "'I got the work done pretty early and went at the ironing. Mr. D did not get home till nearly seven. Hilda is terrible. Mrs. W went downtown. I like Isabel best—God is ever good.'"

Shortly after that, the son of a family she works for drowns in a pond when the ice breaks unexpectedly, and Lucy is let go. It's not clear why, just that it has something to do with the boy's death. Milo surmises that the kid may have died on her watch, walking out over the ice while she wasn't looking.

She decides to move to California, clipping an ad about "Sea and Sunshine" in the "Golden Land of Opportunity" that's still there folded up in the diary. The following summer she takes a train across the Great Plains to Los Angeles and gets a job as a maid for another family in Santa Ana. The entries continue as before.

"'April 23, 1914, knit nearly two fingers on my stocking. Threw down the hay and fed Romeo. We stowed the cistern. Dr. T got me a turkey. I drawed and sugared it. Made a cake and stewed pumpkin and trotted all day and I am tired but happy in God.'"

Milo loves this stuff, thin as it might be on detail. He can spend hours piecing Lucy's life together from the hints she does give, imagining what it must have been like to be around then. Things get really interesting when she meets Edwin and writes about their courtship. She records tea with Edwin's mother after church and horse-and-buggy rides to San Juan Capistrano to see the swallows. Once the two of them take a boat ride to Catalina.

But it ends right after her wedding, with more than half the pages left unfilled. She becomes Mrs. Lucy Kreel, and to Milo it seems as if she drops off the face of the earth. He wants to know how she went from a girl on her own to the wry, crusty old woman he knew as a kid, but he has few clues. She rarely used to talk about herself, at least to him, and since she spent so much time alone, no one who knew her ever had much to say about her likes and dislikes. Milo does know she preferred being alone. That didn't bother her the way it did most people. She could live pretty much how she wanted to. She didn't have to care a snap what other people thought of her.

There are mysteries in the diary that Milo hasn't been able to figure out: X's marking out blocks of days in apparently random order or strings of unintelligible words after an entry. Things like: "TD Winks so-so good solo" or "TD Winks very good chorus." He doesn't understand why she would write in code to herself when it's her own diary.

"Maybe she's afraid someone will read it," Jess surmises.

"Could be," he says doubtfully. "But still."

Jess, feeling heady, watches his limbs with a mind of their own get up from the floor and propel him past Jack's still sleeping figure into the kitchen, where, after stumbling over some medallions, they began to forage through cupboards for food. He finds a bag of chili-flavored Fritos. On his way back, bag in hand, he pauses by the bookshelves and busies himself reading the titles. *Tailspin Tommy in the Great Air Mystery, South Sea Stories, The Long Lavender Look, The Pioneers, The Genius and the Goddess, Adventures in the Skin Trade, Hell's Angels, The Great and Secret Show...*

He chews the Fritos into a pleasing paste on his tongue, swallows a bit and chews some more. He can't seem to stop reading. The books are like hieroglyphs to him. They conceal, in their accidental patterns, an intention to communicate, although what message of accumulation and neglect, interest and the end of interest, he couldn't say. *City of Gold, The Boy's Life of Abraham*

*Lincoln, Blondes Are My Trouble, The Deerslayer, The Space Child's Mother Goose, Men to Match My Mountains, The Last Enchantment, Operating Manual for Spaceship Earth, An Inquiry into the Intimate Lives of Women, The Book of Merlyn, Reality Sandwiches, Delta of Venus, The Threepenny Opera, Five Girls, Skiffs and Schooners, The Adventures of Peter Cottontail, God's Little Acre, Folk Style Autoharp, Longfellow's Complete Poems, Naked Came I, Between Pacific Tides, The Colossus of Maroussi, The Little Shepherd of Kingdom Come...*

"Hey! I think I solved the mystery of the Xs," calls out Milo from the other room. Jess tries to pull himself away from this useless inventory, wondering at the strange pleasure to be had in lists. *How to Keep Your Volkswagen Alive, April Kane and the Dragon Lady, The Medium is the Massage, Craftsmen of Necessity, Grandma's Attic Treasures, Frog and Toad Are Friends, The World Ocean, Candy, A Man with a Maid, The Marvelous Catch of Old Hannibal...*

"Jess!"

He shuffles back into the living room to find Milo still pouring over the diary. "They're not random at all!" he cries. "The Xs happen once every month or so, and come in clumps of four or five. They're for Lucy's period!"

He speaks loudly enough for Jack to stir in his sleep. He groans and turns onto his back. "Are you kidding?"

he mumbles. "All my Jewish friends are lawyers, and all my Italian friends are dead."

Dreams. And words in dreams. Jack is in one of his other nine lives now, exploring other possibilities of memory and desire, of roads taken and not taken, to him they all seem the same.

Milo and Jess wait to see if he wakes up, but he doesn't and they relax again. "I'll be damned," says Milo. "I never once thought it could be her period, not in years of thinking about it."

The two of them contemplate the strange significance of this one-hundred-year-old fact. Mothers' bodies. Women's bodies. Blood and moon. A moon-pulled longing. They both feel it. It's primitive, and it has nothing to do with them, even if they wouldn't be there otherwise. This leaves them both abashed.

Milo thinks of Mariah, his last girlfriend, not so affectionately called the Gray-Haired Lady because her hair had gone all white by the time she turned forty. She was an alcoholic who couldn't ever keep things together. At first it was a lot of fun hanging out with her, but it slowly dawned on Milo that they had to get blottoed every time to make the fun happen. So he put a stop to it. She lived with him in the house for about six months on the condition that she stay sober. And she really tried. But sooner or later something else in her life would happen: her juvenile delinquent kid would get himself arrested for stealing credit cards or her car would break down. Then she'd head straight for the bar and Milo wouldn't see her again till 4 a.m. two nights later, when she'd stumble in all disheveled and mean. He'd try to calm her down, reason with her, cajole her, yell back, coax her into bed, swear this was the last straw, then cave in and give her another chance. He couldn't help it. Sympathy got the better of him. She was low on the East Brother food chain, and that didn't change just because she had the willpower of a tumbleweed.

The final straw came on one of those wretched nights after a binge. She stormed into the house reeking of bourbon and screaming at him as if her fucked up life was his fault. He tried to settle her down as usual, but she tore herself from his arms and flopped onto the sofa... right on top of his violin. There was a loud *POING*!!! and when she rolled over, he saw the neck had been broken clean off. He'd had that violin for two decades. He loved that violin. He'd spent a lot of time learning to get a nice sound out of it, so he could play with his friend Andy on banjo. He stood there agape, the tough cord of his affection cut clean and all the way through. He kicked her out on the spot. He didn't let himself care where she was going to sleep or who with. He shut her out of his heart with a definitive *POING*! She kept coming around for a long time afterward. In fact she still comes around every now and then, ruining his day. He still can't keep any liquor in the house, for fear she'll break in to get it.

Jess, meanwhile, is thinking about a girl he used to know, Lisa Sparling. She worked at the same Home Depot he did and lived in the shadow of a friend who also worked there, a girl everybody thought was glamorous. But to Jess, the friend was vain and transparent and not even that pretty. He urged Lisa not to compare herself or give the friend that power over her, but it was easier said than done. She was self-conscious, being tall and a little rangy, with the kind of blonde hair that was almost red. She also had a small gap between her two front teeth. It didn't make any difference in her looks at all, but it mattered to her. She was saving up money for braces.

Jess liked these foibles in Lisa. They put her at odds with the world and made her a more thoughtful and ironic person to be around. She liked him, too, though they had both accepted that nothing much was going to happen since he'd already enlisted when they met, and before long he'd have to leave. The high point between them was a trip to Newport Beach, where they took a walk by the shoreline, holding hands and talking. That was a good day. They kissed maybe once and that was it. But he felt something deep and abiding for her that he couldn't put into words. All he knew was that it touched on his own solitude and that had never happened before. That made it feel like love.

Milo opens the front door and sits outside on the porch, facing the cypress hedge. He rolls a cigarette. The sky is clear now. Stars dart and blur in the restive branches of the elm trees. Moonlight bounces off Milo's VW. It turns the white siding of the house almost fluorescent blue.

Jess follows him and stands at the edge of the porch with his own cigarette. An eerily backlit spiderweb stretches from the cornerpost to a cypress branch. A huge sun spider sits at the center. Jess lightly touches one of its taut strands, thick as string. The spider tenses up to assess the nature of this message quivering down the pike. Is it prey, or danger? The soft, penetrable flesh of a midge, or sudden apocalypse?

A mockingbird is singing somewhere high up in the elm trees behind the house, a hollow sound in which Milo feels masses of dark air move around him. It's been keeping him awake lately, telling him more than he wants to know about what it's heard on its travels in Mexico: a dog whistle, a car alarm, a squealing hinge, a seagull, a sparrow, a baby hawk. For some reason it has him thinking of how rundown the place is and how much work he needs to do on it. He hasn't been too responsible about that these days. Boards are rotting in the shed out back. Shingles need replacing on the roof. The exterior could use a paint job. He needs to weed and trim. The elms scatter so much seed in springtime that the whole yard would be a forest by New Year's, if he didn't cut the new saplings back on a regular basis. He figures he should devote some time to it, out of respect for Lucy.

But he knows he probably won't. He likes it run-down. Dry leaves, Chinese cabbage seedcases moldering away, scaly paint, scummy trails left by slugs, dirt piles pushed up by moles, baby spiders coming out of the eggs that hang in spiderwebs—Milo's sympathies lie with neglect, with slow ruin, bone salt, rust, pages of old books splotched with mold. His house is a magnet for wildlife: birds, raccoons, and possums all treat the place as an oasis. Old tomcats come there to die, and sparrowhawks leave the yard strewn with the bones and feathers of their prey. He's glad for it. So what if life includes death, maybe even a lot of it? Milo wouldn't have it any other way.

Still, he feels overwhelmed sometimes. The détentes with decomposition themselves decompose, crumbling out from under him. When that happens his whole life seems thrown into fantastic relief, and the choices he's made, even the principles he's made them for, scarily mistaken. Maybe it's all been for nothing, or just nothing, he reflects, the bad dream you get for bad work, and he's living a counterfeit life the same as everybody else in East Brother. On that note he thinks about leaving. He thinks about selling the house to Harry Contento and going north to Santa Cruz, for instance, or south to Mexico. He has a friend who used to work as a secretary for a banana plantation in San Blas, and she's always telling him how great it is down there. He tries to picture himself sitting under the gourd lamps on some veranda, iguanas thrashing around under the house, dolphins riding the waves at sunset time. But it's hard. He can't leave his house. He is his house...how can he leave himself?

This makes him restive enough to ask Jess if he feels like taking a walk. It's warm out, not too breezy, and besides, there's a special show that happens around this time at a place he knows. He won't say more about it than that. Jess says okay, and they head out to Escondido. Milo leads him up into the hills, along streets that curve around white stucco walls, yards embosked with mimosas, and outsized hedges that correct for the irregular contours of the land. No one is around except for them, even though it's just ten o'clock. It feels so hushed and deserted they might be the only people there.

At the top of a wooden stairway they turn onto a street lined with sycamore trees. Jess marvels at the intricate shadows their tangled branches make in the lamplight. Especially interesting are the leaves that fall on occasion around him, floating down to meet their doubles in that netherworld through which he passes.

At length they come to a stone balustrade between two houses, where a dry creek falls from a culvert into a gully. The domed bulk of a hill looms before them, dark except for a row of houses that looks like a string of jewels against its throat. One house in particular, the centerpiece of the necklace, is a three-story cubical building divided into square bays and supported on a row of concrete caissons driven into the hillside. The strange thing about this house, Milo tells Jess, is that it's all glass, even the floors and ceilings. Even the steel spans, pipes, tubing, and ducts of its infrastructure are visible.

"It's totally see-through," he says. "There's nowhere to hide. You can see the clothes that hang in the closets. You can see the furniture from below, through the floor. You can see the wine glasses and plates sitting on shelves in the kitchen. From any one room, you can see what anybody else is doing in any other room."

The house is all ablaze now, and the chairs, tables, computers, spiral staircases, and house plants seem to float in its bright atmosphere. A person is moving around in there, a woman in a white robe, with long golden hair cascading down her back. Milo produces a pair of opera glasses, brought for the occasion, and follows her into a bedroom, where she lays on the bed and flips through the channels on a flat-screen television. That soon bores her, however, so she rises again and coils downstairs to pour herself a glass of wine in the kitchen. She wanders some more through the house, glass in hand.

She ends up in the living room, looking pensively out over the lights of East Brother to the sea beyond. She remains in this attitude for a good while. Then, as if slowly coming to a decision, she undoes the knotted sash around her waist and slips off her robe. All of a sudden she's gobsmackingly naked. Milo, the opera glasses up, tracks her to a bathroom located at the exact center of the house's black rectangular grid, flush against the outer wall.

"She'll take a shower," he predicts. "I've seen it before. She'll stand under the water and touch herself, like Venus in the big scallop shell, in that painting by what's his name."

"Botticelli."

"Right."

Milo hands over the opera glasses. Jess focuses on her before a mirror intently plucking an eyebrow with a pair of tweezers. Brass and porcelain fixtures gleam around her. Angular plumbing snakes away to form the ornamental diversions of the room beneath.

"Imagine," Milo says, "being in the open all the time, with no privacy even in your own bathroom. Who'd want to live like that?"

At this point she does indeed turn on the water in the shower, testing it with her hand until the temperature is right. Steam twists wraith-like up the glass walls but evaporates at once because of a fan built into the ceiling. Jess sees its flywheel spinning in the vent.

"There aren't any upright supports on those steel beams at all," Milo observes. "They must be welded together with fishplates or something, at the joints."

The woman steps under the cascade of water and wets her hair. She soaps herself down with slow flicks of her wrist, lifting one arm at a time to get at the armpits, stooping to slide the soap along the insides of her thighs. Her breasts and triceps quiver as she works shampoo into her hair. Jess sees her look off, wondering if that's the ring of a telephone she hears or the hallucinatory sounds water sometimes makes in a shower. She listens, a smile on her face, and considers getting out to see if she should answer. But the impression fades and she forgets, relapsing into dreaminess. She draws her fingers along the ridge of her clavicle to her sternum. Her head is slightly bent, her lips pursed.

"See!" hisses Milo. "That's exactly what Venus does in the painting. Every time the same thing, man. She must be copying it."

The thought gives him pause. He used to believe it was possible for a woman like her to wander down off her mountaintop and notice him, say, hanging out by the boardwalk, impetuous, idle, his hair tousled, his eyes bright with promise. He'd sense her curiosity, whisper to his friends about the Ice Queen standing there all by herself, and saunter over to say hello. He'd toss his head, bat his lashes, say something folksy about East Brother, and after a while ask if she was interested in taking a walk down the beach to these caves he knew, these eternal caves he always knew. She'd smile, risk vying with fear in her sparkly eyes, before at last yielding to the temptation. In no time they'd be heading to some lonely trysting place by Reef Point.

But that was a long fantasy ago, on the far side of a lot more experience. Now he knows things never work out this way, even when they do sort of work out this way, because the world is just a big glass house with glass ceilings as well as glass floors and glass walls. The sad truth is that woman up there was only ever meant for Milo to look at. She was an idol, or an ideal, against which the women he could know and be around would always pale in comparison. He hates that, but he also wonders if there's a way around it. Maybe a chick in a glass house is all a man is ever really supposed to want in this world. Milo's been known, in times past, to deride his fellow East Brothers for wanting what they can't have, grasping at straws or chasing after rainbows. Maybe, though, he was only running them down to fool himself, to think he was different when he wasn't, when he felt the idol's appeal as much as anybody, no matter how critical or down-to-earth he might claim to be. And with that the fact of getting old presses in on him, brings him up face to face with the illusion inside all other illusions, that there can be some things that aren't illusory. For when the simulations of eternity include even death, you know finally that there really is no escape from living.

Jess is in his foxhole now, tripping on his own thoughts. Being high turns his mind into a show he can watch as if from the outside, like a spectator. He thinks of it as a formal feeling, one that leaves him a person by implication only, there to be filled in by whatever comes his way, at the moment a glamorous naked woman spinning into pinwheels before his very eyes. Yet it could be anyone that fills him in like this, too. That's the weird part. It doesn't matter where he settles his attention because attention itself is what he finds interesting, the way it interacts with what comes into his view more than the things themselves. He blends the woman's body with his, tries out different angles and strategies of copulation—he's only human—but when the shower winds down and Milo suggests they head back, such is his mood that she vanishes again, hardly more lasting than a whim.

## 5

## Nocturne

Near midnight, Milo drags two bicycles from under the Adonis tree and readies them for a trip to the beach. He turns the ten-speed upside down and pumps air into the back tire. Jess squirts oil into the gearwheels of a mountain bike.

"What about Jack?" he asks.

"Don't worry about him. He'll sleep till morning. He always does."

About the only time Milo goes to the beach anymore is at night. No one's there then, and he can approximate those days decades old now when he had the whole beach to himself down by Emerald Cove or on the far side of West Cliff Drive. These days, every strip of sand, every wave, every tidepool is populated, and Milo feels crowded out of his own town.

They wheel the bicycles through the driveway to the street and set out. Milo's removed the ratchets from both of them, so coasting downhill on Escondido, they plunge soundlessly into moony night. The effect is visceral, like butterflies in the stomach. They take their chances at an intersection and pick up speed, flitting rapidly one after the other into a hollow where the road dips precipitously. They surprise a raccoon waddling across the pavement. As they glide by, its round yellow eyes peer after them from under a car.

Escondido straightens as they near PCH, and on the other side it issues into the platted grid of the beach flats. Milo takes the lead and rides south on Paloma Avenue toward Reef Point. They pass a series of streets dead-ending at cliffs. Milo turns into one of these and halts at a sturdy barrier painted white and adorned with reflector lights. They leave the bicycles and head down a flight of spongy wooden stairs, through stands of wild turnip barely visible in the glow of a street lamp.

The beach is overhung with houses built on pillars against the cliffs. Milo strikes out over the sand, and Jess follows after. They pass a rock formation, worn humps of dolomite studded with scallop shell indentures and clam borings. On its far side the beach widens out, feeling more secluded. A while later they come upon a concrete vent with vertical rebar slats in it, the mouth of a creek forced underground somewhere further up. At its base a crater has been scooped out of the sand, filled with standing water.

Milo alerts Jess to the whistle of an onshore wind in the rebar. The sound is eerie and quiring like that an Aeolian harp might make. In it, Milo hears choral voices held endlessly on the same note. Jess imagines a lady out of some medieval romance imprisoned behind the concrete by a sorcerer, rehearsing in her boredom all the overtones of sadness.

"You should hear it when there's more water in the creek," Milo says. "It really gets going then."

They move on, cutting diagonally toward the surf, past an oil drum garbage can and a lifeguard station. The almost full moon pours its pale phosphorescence on the spangled water. The sea unfolds and withdraws, slackens and grows tense. Spent waves layer the beach with their disks of foam. Pieces of kelp washed onto shore huddle in the glow like drowned bodies, surrounded by blue guitar-shaped pools where reflected stars glitter more brightly, it seems, than the stars themselves. Through the rhythmic sonorities of the surf they hear the keening of plovers as they skim the waves. It seems almost too perfect, the foreshortened sea too illuminated, the moon cut from yellow paper, the immense backdrop of the sky only a piece of crinkled tinfoil in some diorama.

"It's El Niño," Milo says as they trail along the shoreline. "That's why it's so sparkly. All this warm water comes from the equator to heat things up, and the red tides bring these micro-organisms called dinoflagellates. That's what we're seeing. When it's warm there's more of them, and they glow in the dark."

Jess bends over the water and sweeps up windrows of foam, releasing them to the breeze.

"You should go for a swim," Milo suggests. "Dive in, come back out again, and shake as hard as you can. Your whole body shimmers."

Jess sees no reason why not. He lifts off his T-shirt and wiggles out of his pants. His lean body shines as white as a sheet. Milo notices a tattoo of a coiling snake on his shoulder. That didn't used to be there.

"You want to go in, too?" asks Jess.

"Naw, you go ahead. I've had my fun. I've already shimmered."

Jess wades into the water, leaps over the first wave, and dives. Then he rushes back to shore and turns himself into a sparkler, a porcupine of light. He goes out farther the second time, just past where the waves break, and lets the current lift him off his feet. He watches the glimmering moonlight on the water, stretched to the horizon, disappear and reappear over the lip of each approaching swell. The lights of East Brother hover in the night like gas in a mercury lamp, down all the way to the boardwalk a mile or so to the west. It's closing time on the boardwalk now, and one by one swatches of colored lights on the rides shut off. Jess massages the water with his arms, pleased by his own buoyancy, by the ease with which he floats.

But then he brushes up against something rough and squirmy that unnerves him a little. He swims back toward shore, and on each downstroke he pushes through what seems to be a large gathering school of fish. He finds his footing in the sand and yells out for Milo, but he forgets his back long enough for a wave to break on top of him. It shoves him roughly into the moiling surf. When he surfaces again, he sees Milo standing knee deep in the water, holding out a hand. The orange gleam of his cigarette hovers in front of his face.

"There's fish," sputters Jess.

"Yeah? So what?"

"Lots of them."

They stand in the shallows and look into the dark underbelly of a wave. Then, with a suddenness that takes even Milo by surprise, the wave turns into a wave of silver fish and crashes around them. The fish wiggle against their calves and splash in the shallow water, hundreds of them materializing out of the foam.

"Grunions!" cries Milo. "Holy shit, man. I can't believe it. I thought they'd been chased out of these parts ages ago."

"What are they doing?"

"Laying their eggs," he tells him. "For some reason it has to be done on land."

Jess kneels down, scooping some up to drop again. Tiny flaked scales glitter prismatically on his hands.

"I haven't seen this many since I was a kid," Milo says. His parents used to belong to a surf club, and on summer weekends they'd go with a bunch of other families to camp at Doheny State Beach. During the day he and his friends would surf, and on nights just like this one they'd wait for the grunions to run. Back then they came by the thousands. The whole beach would be littered with them.

Milo fondly relives those trips. He remembers the hot dog trucks that people converted into vans and used to cook spaghetti and barbecue chicken wings for the kids to eat. Afterward they'd screen surf movies on the sides of the vans with super 8 projectors, and the blue humpbacked waves of Waimea would crash into the balmy night. He and his friends would watch the professional surfers go at it on their John Peele Avenger longboards, slotted way back in the barrel, bowling it or dropping down, right on the nose, grabbing that rail. They'd gossip about their own exploits at the Boneyard that day, recalling the best waves and the worst wipeouts, laughing at some novice who had his board snap back at him on its leash or who broke his skag on the reef paddling out. And, in the background, somebody was always playing Dick Dale and the Deltones. It was a constant. Without Dick Dale, Milo thinks, a profound gratitude welling up in him, those camping trips to Doheny wouldn't have been half so special. Maybe they wouldn't have happened at all. Who knows? Dick Dale, Milo silently affirms to the host of skeptics and naysayers who like to run down surf music, is more than a legend, he's a god. He's a giver of life.

Jess, meanwhile, has slipped still wet back into his clothes. The female grunions are squirming into the sand, making their nests. Soon only their pointy heads and two tiny eyes are visible. The males curve sinuously around them, eager to deposit their milt. Milo, illuminating the spectacle with a raised lighter, is all sympathy.

"They're fish out of water," he quips. "And that's what I've been my whole life, too, so I say good for them. If they want to dig with their tails and lead with their noses, let them."

Jess laughs over the hollow thrum of the waves, struck by just how apt this characterization is. It has them both converging in tacit agreement on the mustiest of proverbs, suddenly freshened, that truth sometimes can be stranger than fiction.

# 6

# The Hash House Harriers

Harry Contento's phone rings at 7:00 a.m. on the dot. He forbids anyone to call before that hour, an interdiction amounting to torture for operatives all over East Brother and outlying areas along the south coast, who, awake since dawn feverishly perfecting his various financial schemes, burn with questions only he can answer. But after seven, the deluge. He rolls over in bed and picks it up.

"Contento," he says.

"Harry, it's me, Harley."

"Hey homey," says Harry, falling onto his back. "Hey bro, what's up?"

"It's Catallus Company, Harry. I'm going through the paces on this general partnership thing…"

Harley, Harry reminds himself, is one of the dimmer bulbs in the light store and not his premium choice for business partners. But since he's also his sister's husband, and blood is thicker than water, he has no choice but to listen as Harley reveals his incompetence one more time.

"No, no, no," he finally interrupts. "Jesus, Harley, how many times do we have to go over this? We buy the hundred acres in Happy Valley with the cash of those ten limited partners you found. You're the agent, Harley. You get 10% of that money. How much is it?"

"$1,346,783 and 17 cents."

"That means you get $134,678 and 32 cents." Harry has a mind for figures you wouldn't believe. "Okay. We're going to have the land timbered by Octagon Lumber, right?" Harry, it just so happens, owns 51% of all stock in that concern. "You get another 10% as the agent for that. We're going to mill the lumber at Gropius"—where he serves as junior vice president in charge of business development—"another 10%. How many percentage points is that, Harley?"

"Thirty."

"Homeboy, it's around two hundred thousand dollars that you've just made as agent here."

"Got that part."

"So what happens next?"

"I bail on the partnership."

"You're on it this morning, Harley."

"But that's where I'm having trouble."

"What trouble?"

"Well, when I bail, I'm going to make those investors pretty angry."

"So?" The irritated syllable swells up like a boil. Harry's five other phone lines are now ringing at once in the background.

"At the end of it, they get a logged piece of property worth a fraction of what they paid for it, and lumber that isn't worth half of their original investment. Most of their money is gone."

"They clear cut what's left and sell. Maybe they get that 50% back after all."

"Like I said, that's going to make those guys a pretty unhappy bunch."

"Harley," says Harry, "you can't worry about what other people think. This is not a weekend at Club Med. It's business. You're a businessman. If you worried about what the other guy thought, you'd never get anywhere."

"It's fraud, right, Harry? I mean, that's what we're basically talking about here, isn't it?"

"Harley, it's not fraud, it's a general partnership. You're not doing anything illegal. If they sue you, they won't have a ground to stand on. Besides, lawsuits are part of the business." Harry is usually involved in two or three at once and, in fact, considers this one of the best indexes of success he knows. "I'd be worried if somebody wasn't suing me."

"But they're all silver-haired retirees, Harry. I like them. They remind me of Ronald Reagan, all of 'em. Patriots. Believers."

There isn't anything Harry Contento doesn't know and revere about believers, but Harley's got his sympathies all turned around here. He tries to set him straight. This happens a lot. A large part of being a diversified entrepreneurial genius, Harry realized a long time ago, is playing the role of teacher for those in his employ less skilled in the art of the deal than he is. He's part dad, part coach, part buddy, easing operatives along in the unfolding drama. It is, indeed, all about belief. Harry could go on for hours about the subject, about the special training he received as a Mormon growing up in Salt Lake, later at Bethany Bible College, and after that as a fledgling real estate agent in San Clemente. But he also doesn't have all day to spend on Harley's moral education here, and philosophical conversations are a youthful indulgence anyway, so before too long he cuts the session short and gets out of bed.

Ah, the euphonious sounds of rings, pulses, clicks on answering machines, beeps, digitized voices! Harry loves it. This is the life, to be wanted by the world at 7:00 a.m. sharp. He goes into the bathroom, swallows a couple of fat reducing pills, then steps through to his atrium and gets on the Nordic Trak. Through the windows he can see the town of East Brother drop precipitously down cascading hillsides to the sea. He wiggles his feet into position, grabs the handles, adjusts the resistance dial, and begins to ski in place.

Harry has cornstraw blond hair and blue eyes. He has a tan so dark and creamy it reminds kids of milk chocolate and enemies of blackface. At forty-five, his skin is a little more gelatinous than before, but he holds his shape and never climbs above 155 pounds without a full-scale regimen of fasts and aerobic marathons down at the body sculpting salon. His stomach is still pretty much flat. He makes a lot of money selling real estate and investing in numerous other miscellaneous business ventures associated with land and resource development. Right now he's discussing Carbondale Homes, a subdivision under construction on the site of an old mining town, into the microphone wedged at his ear. A few malcontent environmentalists are complaining that a rare species of butterfly makes its sole habitat on the pasture land where Harry's building the townhouses. His lawyer, Paul Grass, is explaining to him that they'll probably have to do with one less townhouse and squeeze a butterfly preserve on the lot.

"Fucking socialists," says Harry, skiing, into the phone.

"Then there's a Yorba Linda council member who claims there's not enough of a watershed to support the drinking, garden, and pool needs of the new residents."

"So what?" scoffs Harry. "He's a politician. A Southern California politician! Bribe him."

"We did," says Paul. "He's all for Carbondale now, but we'll have to guarantee the water contracts for the first five years."

Harry has no intention of guaranteeing water contracts, but they can think what they want at this point. Two clicks on the line. He presses the flash button and hears Davey Morecock on the other end.

"Davey, my man! How you doing?"

He listens.

"Oh, that's sweet," he says, "that's cherry." Two clicks. "Hold on, homey. Hello?" It's Ennio, with whom Harry affects a slight Italian accent on account of his background in the Cinque Terra region south of Genoa. They discuss the old person's home he's financing for elderly Italian Americans, who, bored to death in the Everglades, want to live in Temecula because of the wine country and the mountains.

Two clicks. It's T.J. Torrez, his stock broker. "We got Futures Unlimited up to fifty-five a share!" splatters T.J. into the line. He always sounds like he's been running at full tilt.

"Sell," says Harry.

This goes on for the whole forty-minute workout, after which Harry takes a shower, rubs tan preserver lotion all over his body, and proceeds down a stairway of stainless-steel mesh railings and mahogany treads to his Fauve orange library, where he listens to his numerous messages. His house is the one sentimental thing he's ever indulged in. He had it built to his wife Gail's exact Californian ultramoderne specifications. It includes a vestibule with forty-foot ceiling reminiscent of a blast furnace, a large front door made out of beaten brass, a stone fireplace in the round, slanted out Palladium windows, a moat outside, and a pool with infinity edge. He hates it, every deluxe detail, because his wife left him soon after it was finished and took him for practically everything but the house. It still sticks in his craw years later. He's had it on the market ever since the divorce was finalized, but so far no takers at the extravagantly high price he's asking.

He goes through all the messages on his machines, phones still ringing though less frequently now, while he eats a bowl of cornflakes and sips coffee mixed with high-octane brain oil and grass-fed butter. It's the more contemplative time of the morning, when he has a chance to reflect upon his many projects in relative peace. He sinks into his polka-dot red and yellow airblown moonchair next to the hydra-headed spore lamp. Above him hangs a mobile by Alexander Calder. In the bookshelf behind him are collected all the books he owns: *How to Make a Quick Fortune, Reality Bluebook, Talking Straight, Winning, How to Make a Million Dollars in Three Years Starting with No Cash, Franchising: the Inside Story, Dream Your Way to Success, The Apostle's Creed, Highly Effective People, Believe and Achieve, The Negotiating Game, Wealth Without Risk, Nothing Down, Financially Free,* and *Million Dollar Habits.*

One message is from that bastard Ralph Noblefield, a rival broker who's been horning in on Harry's La Jolla territory with a new ad campaign. They've been on shouting terms for years now, and they've hated each other passionately for more years than that. Ralph vituperates into the phone, promising to mack Harry as he has never been macked before in La Jolla. What an asshole. "Noblefield Real Estate. Real Estate is a Noble Field." Okay, okay. Clever. A snappy tag line. But who's going to buy it, even for a second? Real estate is not a noble field. It's a rat race, a cesspool, a tarpit of infinite greed. People aren't stupid.

Not nearly so elegant, thinks Harry, not one bit as classy, as simple, as his own tag line. Noblefield's got nothing on:

Contento Properties, Ltd.
Harold Contento, Community Liaison
IF YOU'RE NOT CONTENT, I'M NOT CONTENTO!

Tried and true, this has been his good luck charm for a decade. It's gotten him where he is today. Because it's straight talk, he thinks. No frills. It says what it means. Of course, his penchant for honesty gets him into trouble. He ends up revealing too much about the soul of Harry Contento. At bottom, he's a chameleon. That's his secret. He's different things to different people. At times in his life, this has even extended to more or less complex aliases he's assumed for the sake of handling all his projects at once and avoiding any perceived conflicts of interest. He used to have ten phone lines going in his house, plus the five at his office, but that got to be too crazy even for Harry, so he's cut back to his present number. His psychotherapist made him promise not to lie to people about his name, his heritage, his age, or his profession, but this has proven too difficult, even if his simulations are much less byzantine than they used to be.

There's a knock at the door. It's Davey Morecock. He never did get back to him on the phone a while ago, but it doesn't matter. Davey's used to it.

"Dude," says Davey. "Let's roll."

"Got a few calls to make, and I'm ready." Today's Hash House Harrier day, and the two of them plan an afternoon of drinking and running with their southwest coast hash chapter.

"Can't be late, Harry. I cannot be late. Elke Anderson's gonna be there, and if she gets a head start on us, I'll never catch up to her." He rolls his alarmingly limber hips and swings his arms, bent at the elbows. "Cuz she's primed and pumped, Captain Chocolate, and I've got a little Davey Morecock to give."

"You horndog," jokes Harry. "You scamdog homey you."

They drive Harry's Porsche to PCH and up Aliso Canyon Road, where today's run through the hills behind East Brother is scheduled to begin. A crowd of revelers has preceded them at the trailhead, and Harry blends in right away, slapping high fives with friends. He takes a swig of his first beer and stretches out. Davey is ogling Elke, a Swede with a shock of blond hair and a torso as long as a giraffe's, while she goes through her warmup routine.

"That chick's Energizer never stops," he says reverently.

Harry notices a recent swelling around the area of Davey's gut. "I don't know, dude. I think you've been breaking the no carb rule on me."

Davey pales. "What do you mean?"

"I wasn't gonna say anything, but...there's a bit more of Morecock than there used to be, you hear what I'm saying?"

"God fucking dammit!" Davey cries. "One day, one order of curly fries and one orange-flavored chicken for lunch, that's all—"

"Like eating two pounds of sugar," observes Harry, shaking his head.

"It's not fair."

"Nobody said life was fair, homeboy."

Davey looks longingly over at Elke. "Do you think she can tell?" he says *sotto voce*.

Harry could care less whether some chick's radar has picked up on Davey's chunky propensities. What worries him more is whether he can rely on his friend to accomplish the special job he needs him for this evening. Davey has been a hatchet man for Contento Ltd. ever since Paul Grass helped him beat a credit card fraud rap a few years back. Davey's the perfect guy for dirty work: dumb and willing. Unfortunately, the dumb part means Harry has to do his thinking for him, which can be a problem if he's not right there by his side, and the whole point of having a hatchet man is that Harry be somewhere else establishing alibis. He hasn't figured out how to install a remote-control device in Davey's brain yet, and until he does, he will have to go with what he's got, which usually means some coaxing, a little sweat, and a lot of strategy. Tonight is going to require special presence of mind on Davey's part, because the work is especially dirty and there won't be much room for error.

Harry calls it The Milo Affair. It started about two years ago, in that casual cupidity so dear to real estate salesmen everywhere. Harry was driving down Josephine Street on the lookout for fresh sales opportunities when he noticed the cottage for the first time. It stood out like the last vacant lot in East Brother, and Harry could already see the house he'd have built there, for some reason (he couldn't say why) in the Tudor style, with slanted beams in the stucco and lattice windows. He stopped the car to investigate and found Milo in the back yard, prone under his apple tree like Isaac Newton, watching the leaves turn red in the light. Harry knew the type: throwbacks, dinosaurs, oddball survivors of a dead time. He'd seen them slowly migrate from East Brother over the years, taking huge profits on properties they'd inherited or bought for a song back in the day and heading for greener pastures. He introduced himself with all the folksy charm he could muster, coaxing Milo out with allusions to a fictitious rural boyhood spent in the Moab desert. He thought he had Milo eating from the palm of his hand when he turned the conversation to the astronomical value of real estate in East Brother and wondered aloud if he might be interested in selling his house. But Milo said no. Harry named a price, lower than it was worth but still more money than he felt sure Milo had ever dreamed of in his life. He still said no.

Harry upped it 25%, 50%, 100%, 200%. Each time Milo demurred.

"I'm not interested at any price," he told him.

Harry was confused. "You mean, you don't care about the money?"

"No," said Milo, with a frown. "I mean yes, but no. I don't know."

Harry left still confident that his new mark could be had, and he kept at him in the weeks and months that followed. Only after Milo said no to pitches and blandishments that would have finagled a cow out of his field did Harry admit he was stumped. He'd never met anyone like Milo before. He contradicted all precedent, all common sense, if not all law natural and otherwise. To Harry, Milo was like saying the sun sets in the morning or gravity only works at the equator. This made the experiment Milo became in the limits of human willpower a test as well for Harry's sense of reality. He wanted to drive Milo to that point of secret greed which Harry assumed to exist in all men even the most virtuous, and Milo, he could tell, was far from that. But he kept on surprising him with his resilience. Finally, when Milo got fed up with the pressure, he had to involve other operatives, going so far as to put a bounty on Milo's head of eight percentage points above commission for the agent who made the sale. He'd also resorted to more devious tactics: threatening Milo through city appraisers and homeowner associations, conspiring with invidious neighbors to make his life miserable, even throwing women at him. None of this worked either. One day, not too long ago, he arrived at the house with one million dollars cash in a suitcase and offered it to him cold-cocked, just to see if he'd take it...and he didn't!

Now, though, Harry has come to the end of his experiment on Josephine Street. At first it was diverting, even fun, to pester the last hippie of East Brother into final surrender. But at some point, in the war of attrition The Milo Affair has become, it got personal. Harry always half-believed the profile others had of him as a man of only one principle, profit, but now he wonders how true that really is. Lately, at any rate, he's come to see a second peek its pesky head from its hiding place in his brain, and it's called property. Milo erodes by his very existence this granite foundation of a free and God-fearing society. Once, during one of his many assaults on Milo's credulity, he remembers him ranting from that sagging side porch, by that creepy tree, about the evils of property. "What are you talking about?" Harry shot back, breaking the rule about clients always being right, at least right up to the point you stick it to them. "Property is the American way!" And Milo answered by saying: "Property eats shit!" Harry could hardly believe his ears. He still can't. The words come back to him like a bad dream, and over time they've taken on the status of a heresy in his mind. This, of course, makes Milo something like the devil.

The run is on. People are downing their beers, their homemade margaritas, their rum and cokes, and starting up the trail. Harry adjusts his headphones and listens to Warren Zevon's *Greatest Hits.* He goes slow at first, pacing himself, waiting for that all-important second wind to kick in. He hardly breaks a sweat before the first mile is up and they stop again for a second round of drinks.

Laughter all around. Fun group of people. Developers, investment bankers, a couple of soap opera actors on the down sides of their careers, but still pretty famous. Harry runs. His head swims a little now. That peculiar cocktail of endorphins and alcohol has its effervescent effect. Things, though less crisp, are more intense. That lizard he just passed isn't sunning itself on a rock but radiating angelic light. That buckeye tree in front of him isn't blooming, it's ejaculating a hundred times over. Zevon's "Mr. Bad Example" sounds positively anthemic in his ears. He always thought that song had potential.

It's been uphill for a while now, but they hit the crest at mile two, stop and drink some more, then run along a ridge trail in view of the ocean. This is the life, Harry says to himself for the second time that day. He's got it made. He cites Matthew 25: "To him who has more, more shall be given, and to him who has not, even what he has shall be taken away." Amen. Thank you, Jesus. Words to pray by. They have him recalling what all in all may have been the most moving experience of his life. It happened in the Philippines. He was on his Mormon mission after Bethany. A friend took him to see a real estate phenomenon named Brother Mike. The guy had managed to persuade thousands of people that he was the next messiah and that the way to ensure election in Heaven was to speculate on housing markets. Harry couldn't believe it. There really were thousands of people who had come to see Brother Mike, this wizened old Filipino who wore gray robes and spoke about meditation and square footage, depreciation and Holy Writ, all in the same breath. But the moving thing that happened came when Brother Mike finished talking, and the whole crowd roared his name in unison. Then, all those people lifted their opened wallets and bankbooks into the air and begged Brother Mike for his financial blessing. Harry felt he was in the presence of God. There was no other way to describe it. Brother Mike was the Lord and that crowd was the Host. The world was one and indivisible, holy right down to its trembling atoms. From that point on, Harry knew what his life course would be: to follow humbly in the footsteps of Brother Mike and combine the good work of real estate with the beneficence of mystical union.

The hash is peaking into that sublime state of intoxication and muscle burn now. The dry baked hills undulate. The horizon tilts. The world swivels. A couple people stop to throw up, but that's okay, it's part of the fun. Hashing is a boom and bust, or binge and barf, experience, a metaphor for life...a religion, thinks Harry, almost. Give and take. Investment and return. Sin and forgiveness. The tide comes in, the tide goes out. Yin and

Yang. Blood corpuscles and sweat. Burn those calories off the microsecond you put them on, like magic.

It took him a while before he connected his early formative experience with Brother Mike to his more recent renewal of faith in the virtues of property. He went through a pretty long period of irreligiousness as a younger man. He hasn't been much of a Mormon; he's been what they call a Jack Mormon. His career in real estate didn't seem to go along with God too well in the beginning. Mormons look down on having fun. That's the one reproach he has of them. They're just not very fun-loving. As a young man, he saw no reason why he couldn't have God and parties, too. That's why he came to California, because he sensed there the possibility of a truer communion with the Lord, hell, a Mormonism truer to itself. But he couldn't really put all this into words. Like everybody else in his life, he just assumed he was moving away from God and embracing the pleasures of the secular world. Only now, so many years and so much experience later, can he make the connection he couldn't then, thanks to his vendetta against Milo. For Milo has taught him all over again that God and property are the same thing, Hallowed Be Their Names! And if that means real estate is the work of the Lord, it follows that real estate agents are ministers, and real estate magnates bishops, even cardinals, of His Word.

Harry has decided this is a lot of responsibility. It's time to act with the dignity proper to his station, and

Milo seems like a perfect place to start. If he thinks property eats shit, he shouldn't be allowed to have property, simple as that. Harry had before understood this only intuitively, hence the half-ass nature of the measures taken up to this point to divest Milo of his property and their continued failure.

He's on top of the world now, hooped by infinite sky. Catalina Island hovers at the horizon right in front of him, like a destination for Olympians. Yes, it's time to stop being half-assed about God, he thinks. *If the eye offends thee, pluck it out.* He has a plan. He looks for Davey at the heart of the hash and finds him next to Elke, grinning at her like a horny baboon. They seem to be hitting it off. Good. Davey needs to be in top form tonight. There's to be an exorcism in the name of justice, terrible and divine. He's to be the exorcist.

# 7

## The Boardwalk

Jess starts awake in Milo's spare bedroom upstairs. It's dawn. A gray light grows in the window and on the wall. Branches scratch against the siding outside. He hears what sounds like a softly shook rattle and a tambourine tapping out a broken rhythm, urgent and near, calm and far away. He hears strung together shells gently shaken, a handful of sand thrown into the Adonis tree, and the tick of a ratchet turned very slowly. It doesn't sound like birdsong at all. It sounds like some hobo orchestra tuning up for a show.

A black cat appears in the doorway. Milo must have left a window open downstairs, because he doesn't have a cat. It stares at Jess with big dilating eyes. Neither of them moves. At length it decides Jess is not going to be a bother and the coast is clear to resume its exploration. It noses into an open closet, temporarily curious about a box of moth repellent that hangs from a hook. It jumps onto a dusty Magnavox TV and peers out the window, its tail twitching to the thought of getting at some of those birds. Not seeing an easy way to do that, it prowls around some more, until satisfied there's nothing else to claim its interest. It finally saunters out again.

Jess follows it downstairs. Jack is still asleep on the sofa. There are leaf-shadows trembling on the closed shades. The birdsong, louder now, almost drowns out the sixty-cycle hum of the refrigerator in the kitchen. Sunbeams slant through the black lattice windows and cast volatile red splotches on the medallions, the spill of oranges in a corner of the counter, the wainscoting above, a framed lithograph of two cows under a tree.

He walks out to the side porch. Periwinkle grows up through the slats and over the worn edge that leads to the back yard. Yellow oxalis blooms around the crab-grass dotted with bowls of standing water, where a few finches splash around until Jess approaches and they fly away. A blue moth flutters in the apple pear tree, which droops like a sad old man. The mock orange laced in the elm saplings is in full bloom. Smilax runs up the gray slats of the shed. Birds of paradise have just opened in narrow slits of livid flame. Carpenter bees hover over holes in the dirt where the planks and glass panels of an old greenhouse sit. Jess turns to watch a russet red dragonfly buzz up and over Milo's eave.

It's like a house in a picturebook. Wood shingles, gabled roof, animals stirring, a warm hearth, time immemorial. It almost doesn't belong in East Brother. It could have been brought in a spaceship from some wet and bygone place and dropped down in Southern

California amid the greasewood and the prickly pear, the freeway and the commercial strip. It's a long way from North Island and the Navy, that's for sure. He'd be in his uniform by now, up to his elbows in dishwater. Chugging away across the Pacific. He feels a stab of remorse at the thought, but it's more a dream to him than reality, a bad dream from which he's glad to awaken. He tries not to let it upset him. The moment is too perfect and the contrast too sharp. He'll figure out what to do about his fucked up life later. Now he just wants to be here, in this other dream.

His mom used to visit the house as a kid, too. But she never liked it. She found it gloomy. It reminded her of dead people and a past she had no interest in preserving. She wanted life to be sunny and bright, future-looking, Tomorrowland not Frontierland. He has to admit the house gives him the creeps sometimes. It sags like a spiderweb laden with dust. The problem is, the future feels just as weighed down to him, even if in a different way. Plastic siding impervious to rot or rock gardens instead of grass carry with them their own burdens of accumulated ache. He knows it, and so does his mom, deep down. She's never been happy in that aseptic ranch house Jess grew up in, though she would never admit it. She deals with disappointment by denial, which pushes her a little more each day into the excessively tidy half-light of a secret bitterness. Jess has had to live there, too, coming by slow degrees to terms with a lack of warmth in her and in their life together that would keep him feeling ill-at-ease in his own skin right up to the present. Not that his mom's especially cold-hearted. Just the opposite in fact. She has a well-deserved reputation for looking on the bright side. Her bitterness isn't personal, that's the thing. It has nothing to do with other people, but with an absence in herself she can't abide any more than she can change, and which he sometimes sees troubling her as she cooks dinner or sews slipcovers to match her curtains or insists his dad place his glass on a lace doily. In the very rituals of a life she had been led to understand would be a consolation and a reprieve, that absence in her grows ever wider, as if there were a precise inverse relation between them, and she's never been able to figure out why.

Since he should be washing dishes anyway, he decides he might as well do Milo's from last night. He returns inside, fills the plastic tub Milo keeps under the sink with hot water, and sets to work. That's how his uncle finds him when he later appears bleary-eyed and disheveled, rubbing his jaw because of his toothache. He slept fitfully all night, waking up in cold sweats while the nerve in his gums throbbed.

"You're up early," he says.

"It's habit."

"I bet they roust you out first thing in the Navy." He reaches in by Jess's waist to fill a pot with water, steps over to the stove, and lights a burner to make coffee. After that, he sits down at the table and rolls a cigarette.

"How long'd you say you were staying for?" he asks casually.

"Till tomorrow sometime. That's when I have to get back to base."

Milo nods, preoccupied with his rolling paper and tobacco. They hear a groan and a thump in the living room. Presently Jack the Cat comes in to join Milo at the table.

"Didn't know where I was when I woke up," he says, smacking his lips.

"That's the loneliest feeling in the world, waking up someplace and not having any idea how you got there," says Milo.

"I've woken up that way more times than I can count," says Jack. "I wake up that way in my own house."

Jack's house is currently a derelict mental health hospital on Bearded Willow Road. No one used the place, so he went ahead and moved in. He set up his tumblers in the day room, turned the cafeteria into a warehouse, and made his bedroom one of the isolation chambers. It's so full of his various glass products that he calls it the Crystal Palace. But he doesn't particularly like it there. Bad karma. He'd prefer to get the glass business going strong again so he could use it just for that, and rent his own place.

"What time is it?" he asks abruptly.

Milo takes out his favorite pocket watch. "7:45."

Jack leaps to his feet. "Holy fucking shit!" he cries. "I gotta be at the clinic by eight. That's when they dose!" He races out the side door and vanishes like the wind.

"See you later, Jack," says Milo drily. "Hasta la vista."

A lot of addicts have come and gone through his house over the years, a lot of possessed people. He's listened to it all, the rants, the excuses, the lies, the sadness, the desperation. He's an addict expert. He even has a theory about it. Whatever it is that possesses them, drink, a drug, sex, Milo sees the same need to act without thinking, without reasons. That's not a bad thing, when it's instinct, which is to say a natural aptitude or impulse that combines emotion and logic. Most people don't see instinct this way. They equate it with emotion and leave the logic out. But for Milo, emotion by itself is too stupid to be instinct. If instinct were only emotion, it would never get what it wants. Of course, it's not just logic either, even if it needs what logic offers, because by itself the logical mind would never want anything at all. Both have to go together on his account.

People equate instinct with addiction, too. Milo, however, after sitting where he is now and listening to husbands climb walls out of jealousy, shellshocked Vietnam vets tell stories about Search-and-Destroy missions, and sad rejected lovers tormented by some specific Beatrice they can't forget, knows better. Addiction is a perversion of instinct. It might want the same thing and have the same energy, the same drive, but it lacks the right balance of emotion and logic. Instinct is graceful, not compulsive. It's a leaping tiger, not a crazed monomaniac.

Milo explains his theory to Jess over coffee and cigarettes. "We get to instinct a couple of ways," he says. "We get there by accident first off. That's an orgasm, say, or drugs—anything that shoots us on up. We don't need logic then. It feels good and we just want more. But what happens when we can't get that feeling? Then we need logic to come around and say, 'now you have to do this and this to get it.' You have to plan. There has to be a purpose."

Jess thinks back to that acid trip with Chris, to how completely he'd lost his head and yet how little scared he really was. The high never tipped into panic. He didn't know what he was doing or even who was doing it, but he didn't not know either. Whatever $n^{th}$ dimension he'd entered and however disorienting it might have been, he felt at home there—at least he did up to the end, when he returned to base. It did get scary then. But in the best part of the experience he had another kind of control going, something he couldn't even call by that name maybe. He wasn't in control, but there was control. This, he takes it, is what Milo means by instinct.

"Right," Milo says, on hearing Jess try to make this connection. "Dope is never a haze with me. It's not about running away from life. If anything, it's about facing up to life, about going more deeply into whatever it throws at you." He turns over the piece of paper with the cormorant on it and draws a line in pencil. "It's like this here line is life, right? You plug along, maybe like a wave"—he overlays it with a sine curve—"and with a little dope you can drift off around by where it hits its peak or where it comes down again at the trough. That's what I'm talking about. It doesn't matter which it is: the high or the low. You can riff on both...."

They fall silent in consideration of the riff, the screaming guitar solo, the bluegrass breakdown, the aria, the moment beyond hope or fear when something unequivocally slays. Both feel a bit sheepish, though, as if paying homage like this betrayed some qualm or scruple they can't quite admit in themselves.

Milo knows its sources well enough. He knows the fear holding him back from that moment, from the full, intense life he's always wanted for himself. He has no one but himself to blame and no real appetite for excuses either, but it makes him mad, too, because he knows it isn't only his fault. "The thing is you can't ride that wave alone," he says. "You need people to help you get off without fucking up. A tiger has other tigers to be around. He has a whole environment. Put him in with a bunch of crazed monomaniacs and he'd lose his instinct, too." He takes a last drag of his cigarette and flings it back behind him into the sink. "Look at me and cigarettes. One right after the other. You think I don't know that? Everyday I'm staring at them saying, 'Let me go! Let me go!' But I can't do it. I need that crutch, that support, and why? Because the environment is messed up, and that means I'm messed up. There's no separation. We are the environment. We're not in it. I hate when people don't get that. They think all we are is individuals doing our own thing, pulling ourselves up by our bootstraps. Bullshit. It ain't fucking true."

A knot slips tight in Milo's mind, turning his thoughts into Gordian paradox. And just as quickly all the disparate elements of his life assemble themselves into patterns on the far side of knowing. Everything's related and nothing's related. God dammit! He wants another cigarette...and maybe a couple of aspirin for the toothache. He's noticed that the two together make the pain go away.

Jess senses his uncle's mood has soured, so he suggests they do something fun, like go to the boardwalk. Milo groans. That's the last thing he needs. He hates the boardwalk. He mumbles about having to touch up his medallions, clean the house, replace shingles on the roof. But each reason only perfects the image he sees in Jess's eyes, of someone who prefers to hang back and feel sorry for himself. He doesn't like that image. Jess doesn't need it now. He needs a bitchin' guy. He therefore changes his mind and says, "Oh, what the hell. Let's go."

He rolls a few cigarettes to put in his shirt pocket, and they take off for the beach flats on their bikes. It's a gorgeous sunny day, clear enough to make out the meadows and bluffs of Catalina Island far away. Down on Del Mar the crowds are already miasmic. The boardwalk promises to be packed all the way till midnight. Milo feels what he calls The Great Reluctance steal over him as they head into the shadow of the roller coaster. The people come from inland suburbs, tract-house wastes, aglow with a strange tribal fire. Mall rats, hip-hop dudes, skate punks, chollos—to Milo, they're all barbarians moiling at his gate.

They lock the bikes up at a rack outside the front entrance. An arch in vague Zen Buddhist style leads to the central esplanade, with rides on both sides, except where it opens onto the beach and a detached stage for open air concerts. They merge into the stream of funseekers, heading toward the massive Ferris wheel. Ramps go up to a second level, where you can get on the gondolas that float overhead and afford opportunities for evil-minded kids to spit on the crowds below. Rides swirl like waterspouts, grope like octopus's arms, levitate like swamis all around them. Colored lights blink, slash, bloom, and pulse. People swerve and glide, given over to the tender ministrations of machines. The roller coaster cars swoop down beneath the promenade, trailing screams of terror and joy after them, wringing all but the last ounce of the human from their riders.

Milo feels queasy. He knows why: the smells of stale popcorn, hot dogs, and salty pretzels. More than once he ate too much of that crap and regretted it. He wishes he could say he's since learned his lesson. He knows, though, that the queasiness isn't so much a triggered memory as an anticipation, a forgetfulness of the past that is the secret of all doubling down, all coming back for more. He has a theory about that, too.

"Life boils down to three things," he declares as they thread through the crowd.

"Three things?"

"That's right: candy, gravity, and hormones. The three essentials, man. They'll never change. Give a guy those three things, and he'll obey you forever."

Jess takes his point but thinks now might not be the best time for philosophizing. "Hey, you want to go on the merry-go-round?"

Milo doesn't want to, no. "Sure, why not?" They purchase tickets and wait in line, watching the various animals rise and fall around the center pole, to the hectic sounds of a calliope. There's mirrors everywhere, reflecting riders, rounding boards, brass drop rods and sweeps, couchant angels tooting their gilt horns.

"Is this one you worked on, Milo?"

"No, this is a classic. A Looff carousel. From 1911. Beautiful, huh?"

On the clang of a bell, the carousel grinds slowly to a halt. People file out the exit, and the gates open for new riders. It's always a race for the outermost seats, since on them you can take metal rings from a dispenser to throw at the open maw of a clown's head as the carousel swings you by. Milo shoulders his way past a couple of kids and a bossy mom to snag an Arabian horse with a long curved neck and cut-glass jewels for eyes. Jess gets a griffin right beside him. They wait a minute for the other seats to fill, and an attendant rings the bell. With a drawn out creak the platform lurches forward and the calliope shudders on. They start rising and falling. Milo throws a ring at the clown. He misses. The carousel gains in speed, working itself up to a pretty fast jaunt. Hands are soon grabbing at the dispenser one right after the other. Rings thwack against the canvas surface on which the clown's head has been painted. Before long someone with luck or a surer aim hits the mouth and it lights up.

Afterward they resume their vagabondage down the boardwalk. The carousel's roused Milo from his torpor. He's back in the swing of things, looking around with that keen scrutinizing gaze of the local. They come to the Wave Jammer. He notices an acquaintance of his, Simon, who works in the boardwalk art shop, painting a new backdrop for the ride.

"Look at that shit," says Milo. "That's the worst beach scene I've ever seen." He's never liked Simon, and he's feeling ornery, so he walks over to harangue him about the work he's doing.

"What kind of a painting is that?" he calls out.

Simon glances over his shoulder as he models the cabled throat of a surfer, who resembles a younger version of himself: blonde shaggy hair, a tan, square jaw, a winning smile.

"What do you mean what kind of painting?" he says, blinking. "It's a painting."

"Don't you have any sense of value?" Milo says.

"Value?" He steps back and takes in the whole scene. "I think the values are pretty damn good there." He points vaguely at the sky.

"But there isn't any separation, Simon. The blue in that sky isn't any different than the blue in the surfer's shorts, or in that wave he's riding."

This makes Simon mad. "You're such a grump, Milo. You don't have to like it. I'm not painting it for you anyway."

"All right, all right," says Milo. "I just thought you might want a little advice, that's all." They shuffle off again, and he says to Jess: "I don't know how that guy thinks he can call himself an artist. He can't even get his horizon to fall back right. What a Neanderthal, man. A cave painter. It's artists like him who ruin the place for me. It's all gone to pot. I don't see the nice little touches that used to be here, like pinstriping on the cars and hand-painted decorations on the signs. They've gotten sloppy."

There's a strut in Milo's walk that Jess recognizes from his Navy buddies. It suggests a manhood more wolfish than normal for being so long cooped up. Milo's eyes rove and his tongue starts moving fast in his mouth. His eyes brighten as a girl in a red crop shirt sashays by.

"Whoa!!" he says, turning back around to appreciate her long-limbed gait. Jess, he notes, doesn't follow suit. He's otherwise distracted by the lights and motion, lost in the moment. "Did you see that?"

"Yeah."

"Her tits were so firm and round they looked liked pomegranates in her shirt."

"I love pomegranates."

"All I wanted to do was eat them."

"Maybe you should've talked to her, Milo."

"Are you crazy? I'm way old, man. What would she want with a guy like me? *You* should've talked to her."

Jess is a pretty good-looking guy, Milo thinks. He should be chasing his dick all over this town. God knows Milo's done enough of that in his time. But Jess doesn't seem all that interested. He never has, when it comes down to it. Jess's always been a little too spacey for his own good. You might even think he was slow on the uptake because of it, if he didn't surprise you every now and then with insights that showed he was taking things in, listening from whatever distant place in his head he happened to be. No, it wasn't lack of intelligence you sensed in Jess. If anything, it was too much. Life was just too complex for him. He was always struggling with that. And as frustrating as this might be in a person, Milo see no reason why it's not a virtue at the end of the day. Better than missing out on how complex life is, like most people—usually because they're busy chasing their dicks all over town.

They approach the bumper car ride. It's mostly girls and older women standing around, mothers waiting for their kids to finish crashing into one another. Milo wanders off on his own, aroused by their proximity. Soon Jess spies him across the rink, standing behind a tall girl with a fake fur coat on. Milo sidles in behind her, till his chin almost rests on her shoulder, and he glances sideways to get a look at her face. She has no idea what's happening. Jess laughs.

"What's so funny?" says a voice next to him.

He looks down at a girl about twenty, with spikey bleach blonde hair, a button nose, and pale freckled skin. She wears a boy's paisley shirt with a stiff pointy collar and bellbottom pants.

"My uncle," Jess says. "He's trying to pick up chicks."

"That's what you do by the bumper cars," she says matter-of-factly. "It's a cruiser's paradise."

"Are you cruising, too?"

She ignores this. "What's your name?"

"Jess."

"I'm Olive. Olive Moll."

"That's a cool name."

"I know, I know," she protests. "Don't tell me. You're thinking, gun moll. She's a gun moll. That's the first thing every guy says. I hate it."

"I wasn't thinking that."

"Yes, you were," she counters. "Don't deny it. Men are all the same."

No words in his or his sex's defense pop into Jess's mind here, so he sways on his feet and watches the bumper cars.

"You're a real talker, aren't you?"

"Sometimes I can't think up things to say."

"Yeah, well, I'm not one of those girls who's going to do all the work, for your information."

"Where are you from?" he offers.

"Chicago."

"Where all the gangsters are?"

"That's right." She likes this retort. "What are you doing?"

"Hanging out with my uncle."

"Guess you're busy then," she says, starting off again. "Be seeing you."

"Wait!" She pulls up short and swings around. "I'm not doing anything special."

"Oh," she says. "Me neither."

Just then Milo appears again.

"Hey, Milo."

"Jess."

He introduces Olive, who acknowledges him with a sulky glance. Milo sniffs out the situation at once. He almost thinks he knows Olive from before, but it's just her type he knows. Scruffy beachtown kid who's always been at the boardwalk. There's an awkward silence. "We were thinking of...taking a walk," Jess says, "the two of us."

Milo knows the code by heart. Time to fade away. "You go on. I got plenty to do."

"I'll catch up with you later."

"Sure thing."

Moments later, Jess finds himself accompanying Olive back down the boardwalk. She threads her way too fast through the crowd, keeping him on his toes. They walk like this to the other end and pass under a covered gallery that leads to a video arcade. She goes on about her name.

"I hate it," she says. "Olive Moll. What kind of a name is that for a girl? I feel cursed by that name."

"I like it."

"It's too close to Olive Oyl. That's the second thing every guy says about it."

They pass the store with the machines that blow cotton candy into big swirls and stretch taffy on shuttling racks. Then they go into the arcade, past the foosball tables and the shooting gallery. They stop at an antique Kinetoscope and take turns peering through the magnifying glass at the eerie flickering lope of a camel in the desert. After that, they go to the platforms for the virtual reality games. People stand with the headsets on and twitch edgily. The lines are too long for Olive, so she leads him to the pinball machines in back. She gravitates to one in particular and inserts some quarters.

"This is my favorite," she says. "We can play doubles."

On the backglass is an animated man in a ten-gallon hat racing through a desert landscape, pursued by a posse of rangers. Jess can't believe it. The man looks just like Jack the Cat. The game, in fact, is called Cactus Jack, and the idea, apparently, is that the player tries to catch him or hit him with a ball, but he always gets away. Olive presses the start button, a hectic music erupts, and Jack the Cat's voice says: "He-he-he-he-he! Ha-ha-ha-ha-ha! Geeeeettt ready for Cactus Jack!"

"I know that guy," says Jess.

"Everybody knows him."

"No, I mean I met him."

"You did not!" cries Olive, as she shoots the ball into the playfield. She starts racking up points, hitting drop targets and spinners.

"Yesterday."

"Fuu-uuck you!"

"It's true."

"Liar!"

The ball swings in a wide arc toward the right out lane. She presses her hip against the machine and jerks it. The tilt sensor comes on and the ball bounces placidly between dead flippers. She makes way for Jess.

"Next thing you'll be telling me you chill with Jesus," she says. "Or Madonna. Or Bon Jovi."

"He's real, I swear. He's getting over a heroin habit, he sells glass for a living, and his liver's shot."

"Get out of here! Jack's a god, man. He's up there with the angels. See?" She lifts her paisley shirt to show her belly button, pierced brutally with a stainless-steel barbell. On her abdomen is a tattoo of a red cat's head. It has yellow eyes and yellow whiskers, and its mouth is opened to reveal sharp yellow fangs. Printed on its forehead are the words "His Way," with the left column of the "H" forming an arrow pointed up. "He doesn't have a liver. He doesn't have a body."

Jess kicks the ball up a rollover and it disappears into an eject hole. The machine goes silent for a second, and Jack's voice erupts in an evil cackle. "Heeeerre we go again!" he cries, as bells start ringing and two balls pop into the playfield. Jess struggles to keep them going, but the change unnerves him and he loses both in short order. Olive is not impressed.

"You and Jack must be pretty tight all right," she cracks.

This turns out to be the beginning of much ribbing on Olive's part. Jack actually is a legend in East Brother, a byword among the disreputable, a figure of longing and clairvoyance for all the transitory riff-raff. As Olive and him make the rounds of the boardwalk over that day, playing more games in the arcade, riding the roller coaster, spitting on passersby from the high gondolas, listening to a guy who looks like a pudgy John Denver sing sentimental love songs in James Taylor's exact voice during the lunchtime concert, Jess notices the signs of his fabulous absence. He sees "Jack Lives!" graffitied above the urinal in the men's bathroom, a rampant Jack the Cat tagged on the gunite concrete embankment of the Placitas Creek where the boardwalk terminates in a look-out, a topiary tree of Jack holding up his hand in the Vulcan gesture of salute, plaster figurines of Jack in novelty stores, stuffed animals with shirts that say "I" and "Jack" inside red hearts, a special pizza slice in his honor on the menu board at Fat Apple's, and so on. Jess wonders why he never noticed this omnipresence of Jack at the boardwalk before. Now that he's looking for it, he can't not see it.

But he stands his ground with Olive and swears Jack the Cat is a flesh and blood person. It becomes a running dispute between them, carried on at the top of the Ferris wheel, on the deck of a pirate ship, in the belly of a yellow submarine. It helps put them at ease with each other, although Olive never loses a sarcastic edge that Jess can see comes from a streetwise life. She's been a juvenile delinquent for years, driving her mom crazy and breaking records for time spent at the local Youth Authority. She's been arrested for everything from violating curfew to drunk and disorderly conduct. She's on a first name basis with most of the East Brother police department.

"I figure I better live while I can," she says, "because I don't plan on hanging around past thirty-four. If I'm still alive at thirty-four, I buy a bottle of pills and check out."

"Why thirty-four?"

"That's how old my mom was when I was fourteen."

"What happened when you were fourteen?"

"Nothing. That's just when I realized what a loser my mom was. I swore then that I'd never end up an ugly wet rag like her."

They make their way to the beach. Olive carries a paper bag with a pint of Bacardi 151 they bought from a liquor store on Del Mar, and Jess bangs a pack of cigarettes against the palm of his hand. They go underneath the boardwalk past shifty Mexican kids selling marijuana in the shadows. Olive leads him through pilings to a spot she likes beside a ring of stones with charred wood inside. They sit. Olive downs swigs of the rum like a guy might. Jess smokes. The boardwalk thunks and rattles and occasionally roars over their heads.

"You think I'm good-looking, huh?" she says presently.

He takes her in with frank, unswerving eyes. "You're all right," he teases.

"Good enough to fuck anyway."

He doesn't answer, but he's wondering whether the freckles on her face and throat travel down to her shoulders.

"I've always been a tomboy," she says. "Guys go for that nowadays."

"Some guys don't."

"Older guys especially. They like poking little girls. I can tell, when they're doing it, that that's what turns them on. I remind them of a kid."

"Maybe girls like doing it with their dads."

"Never had a dad, so I wouldn't know."

How many guys has she taken down here? Jess wonders. He figures the answer might surprise him. And with that he feels suddenly distant, or split in two, as if a part of him had left his body behind to look at the other part with Olive in the sand, talking and pretty soon fooling around, too, as she sinks into his arms and kisses him with the same willful extravagance she does everything else. It feels unreal when her bony alleycat's chest presses in against him. His hand passes as if through her waist, through the musky shimmer of her force field. He wouldn't call the experience bad. He has fun rolling around with her, getting sand in his hair, laughing as she does with lips pressed firmly together. But the truth is he's only half there. Maybe he's only ever been half anywhere.

Right then the most definitive proof of Jack the Cat's celebrity staggers past in the form of a crazy man heading into the darkest underbelly of the boardwalk. Olive wiggles out from Jess's arms and attends him with curious eyes.

"Who's that?" he asks.

"A guy. He hangs around the neighborhood. Let's follow him."

She springs to her feet and walks off. Jess runs to catch up, following her into a pitch blackness relieved only by one slanting ray of light from a drain or broken in slat above. That's where the man has gone. He sits in the small circle of light it spills onto the sand, raving. He wears a soiled blue satin jacket with elastic cuffs and the insignia of a bowling team stitched with red thread into the breast pocket. His greasy hair is matted to his temples. His leathery face is riven and mottled in the cheeks. The bones sharply protrude beneath his skin.

He keeps repeating the name Jack. "Calm down, Jack. It's not the end of the world." An eerie, suspirious laugh follows. "Jack's here, I know he is. Jack Sprat can eat no fat. Jack is Jack. Jack is Jack, Jack-is-Jack. All work and no play make Jack a dull boy. He-he-he." He turns gruff. "Hey Jack, how's it going?" He glances sharply off as if to a buddy. "I think Jack's lying. Jack's got a mind, you know. Jack's a liar, Jack-the-lad. I know you're here, Jack. You don't know jack, Jack. Nope, Jack's here. Here, here, and here again. So many chicks think I'm the jack. Oh Jack, Jack, Jack. Beat off Jack. What kind of a man would say jack of him? It's time for Jack. Goddam Jack! I don't care jack for you or your old lady. Ain't that right, Jack? I won't cop to it. What are you gonna do, ball the jack? Jack-the-lad? Huh? Ball the jack? You don't say? I'll give you a dollar for a buck, Jack. You know it's no big immature problem. Ball the jack, ballthejackballthejack. I don't even know what time it is."

He glances over his shoulder and flashes smiles at potential eavesdroppers as he speaks. He seems fantastically isolated in that weird beam of light, a wounded apparition, a vision of the night.

"Gimme some jack, Jack. Got some Jack? Have you been jacked today? Fuckin' A, Jack, is that a fact? I believe in Jack, don't you?"

He searches for some hint of a rhythm or a counterpoint in that name, conjuring an interlocutor from the hard kernel of its mystic monosyllable. He rolls it in his mouth, over and under his tongue, sucking on it as if to make a world out of nothingness itself. His mad figure, to Jess's eye, overspills its boundaries, stains the space around it, appears halated against the darkness, a verbal halation, a word made visible and overflowing. But at the same time he's not there, as neutral and anonymous as the name Jack could ever be, his presence a kind of rarefaction to whose curious phases Olive and him bear astonished witness.

"You got a few idiots sure like to lick the lollipop, Jack. Ain't it a shame? Sure, Jack, you got that right. Jack it up, Jackson, Jack's got some jack he'd like to jack himself off with. Don't worry. You won't get jack for it..."

Olive has been edging closer, till the man senses her there, a silhouette against the band of ocean light behind. A roller coaster car careens over its tracks somewhere up the boardwalk.

"Hey, Rufus," she says. "It's Olive. Remember me? I'm the little girl who lived in the teardrop trailer. Behind Marelina's. You used to read *James and the Giant Peach* to me on your stoop, before you bugged out."

He gapes at her as if he can't quite believe in her presence there, even less sure to him than his own. But he begins to remember the little girl she's talking about, lost way back in his blasted mind, and he doesn't react with anger or fear. She has an ability to put him at ease. She creeps in even closer.

"Is that *The Book of Jack*?" she asks reverently, pointing at a pocket-size volume he holds in his lap. The same red cat's head as Olive's tattoo adorns the front cover. He peers down at it as if dumbfounded. "I've never seen one before. Everybody keeps it so secret. Can I look at it?"

She eases herself down by his side and tugs it gently from his grasp. She opens its covers and turns the hallowed pages. She calls Jess over from where he hangs back in the darkness. He comes to kneel by her side. "You have to be initiated into the Order to have one of these."

"What Order?" whispers Jess.

"The Order of Jack, dummy. Members are called Protagons. Nobody knows who they are. They lead normal lives, except every Saturday night they wear these cat masks and meet in front of the Rio theatre, after *The Rocky Horror Picture Show* lets out. They perform magic rituals with dice and cards and amulets. They're the Keepers of the Book."

The Book is a collection of stories, anecdotes, apocrypha, and words of wisdom written from Jack the Cat's perspective and organized by chapter and verse. Cheaply printed, more like a chapbook, this copy has been much fingered and dogeared. The pages are smudged and spotted with mold. Olive flips rapidly through them.

"Slow down," Jess says.

"You can't read it! You're not one of the Keepers. Only they can read it without going crazy. That's what happened to Rufus."

"I want to anyway," he insists.

She reluctantly stops at the fifteenth chapter as Jess reads:

How Jack the Cat got his name

*15  I was living up in Big Sur, way back in the early days, about a year before I came to East Brother. ²I rented this shack from Iryna the Witch. ³She was this old Russian countess with long white hair that had these little braids in it. ⁴And she had all these little Russian chickens with the same long white hair and the same little braids in them, which were always flying around.*

*5  She really was a witch, too. A water witch. ⁶She carried with her this huge tuning fork that she'd hold over the ground till she felt it vibrate. ⁷That meant the water table was high right at that spot, and you could sink a well there. ⁸People would pay her money for that.*

[9]*Anyway, she owned this land that you had to pass through to get to a place called Badass Canyon.* [10]*You had to go up this spur from her house and around this saddle, way the fuck up there, but it was perfect for growing sensimilla.* [11]*So me and my friend Andre snuck up and put in a few hundred plants.* [12]*Whenever we went to check on them, we'd tell Iryna we were going for a hike.* [13]*And she always believed us, even when she saw us with these cannisters of tiger piss on our backs, which we spread around the patch to keep the deer away.*

[14]*So it came time to harvest, and we had to carry it down in small batches, so she wouldn't know what we were doing, and manicure it in my shack.* [15]*One day I'm waiting for Andre to show up with the last batch from Badass Canyon, pouring warm honey water on the bales we got.* [16]*Suddenly I hear gunshots.* [17]*I go outside and see Andre running for me, and then I see Iryna the Witch with a .45 in each hand.* [18]*She aims one right at me and fires.* [19]*BLAM! I take off.* [20]*My VW van is parked down the road, and we tear ass straight for it.* [21]*But as we do I see four or five scruffy guys come out of these trees.* [22]*They looked like they'd been living in the woods for weeks, and it turned out they were undercover cops working for the DEA.* [23]*Anyway, they run after us, too.* [24]*We hop into the VW and take off down the road, but more cops start following us in these trucks, and they're gaining on us fast.*

[25]*"Motherfucker," cries Andre, "they're gonna catch us."*

*26 The road that leads down from Iryna's house starts to switch back at one point, which means you have to zigzag down this hill. 27So I'm driving up on the first zig, and those DEA guys are right behind us, trying to shoot the tires out on the VW. 28I take the turn a little too fast, and before I know it the van's tilting over the side and spilling down the hill. 29It felt just like the car was doing somersaults. 30I had my hands on the wheel with the gas pedal floored, and I'm looking out the window at this topsy-turvy world. 31Then, suddenly, I have this feeling that nothing bad can happen to me. 32It's like I'm immune to all catastrophe. 33We tumble into the road where it switches back, and the car keeps on falling down that hill. 34We tumble into the road still further down, and it's the same thing. 35The whole time Andre's screaming his head off. 36But when we come to the bottom of the hill, the van hits the main road on four wheels and BAM, we screech off just as if nothing's happened! 37The cops are still way up on the hill negotiating those hairpin turns and we're burning rubber down to Highway 1 and a hiding place. 38Andre looks at me like I'd just parted the Red Sea.*

*39 "Holy fucking Jesus H. shitkicking Christ, you are the luckiest cat I have ever seen," he says. 40"I'm sticking close to you from here on out." 41And from that moment on he started calling me Jack the Cat, because he said I always landed on my feet.*

Jess stops there. It's Jack all right. He wonders if he knows about his Book, or about the Protagons, or about His Way on Olive's stomach. Probably. But it probably doesn't matter either. Jack's a person who got so big he forgot himself. A strange fission took place, like one molecule becoming two, and both identical, so you couldn't tell anymore which came first. Jack has a double that's so powerful it makes him the double of his double, a copy of a copy. That he has a liver, or that he has to eat and sleep and live somewhere, or that he might have needs and cravings of his own, all seem beside the point, details that kick around an alternate universe, like information in a huge database with no search engine. They might as well not exist even when they do.

Olive turns the pages some more. Jess reads other titles in the top margins: "The seventh miracle," "'You shall not eat blood,'" "Vampires in the tenements," "Paranoid pot," and "Jack slays 7000 men." There are appendices of chants, mantras, lamentations, and psalms, all about Jack the Cat. And at the end there's a sermon called "Acedia and Tristetia," by someone named Anti-Climacus. Jess catches Olive's wrist and reads this snippet: "The hand of the LORD was upon Jack, and he brought Jack out by the Spirit of the LORD, and set Jack down in the midst of the valley; and it was full of bones. And he led Jack round among them; and behold, there were very many upon the valley; and lo, they were very dry. And he said to Jack, "Prophesy to these bones, and say to them, 'O dry bones, hear the word of the LORD...'"

Olive wrests her hand free and turns the page. "You better watch it, dude. If a Protagon finds out, you're history."

The crazy man has meanwhile been rocking back and forth, muttering his random invocations of Jack. Now he tenses up and points. Terror spreads in his face. Turning, Jess and Olive see a large billowing shadow bear down on them, and it has what appears to be the head of a brontosaurus. "Heeeyaaggghhhh!" the crazy man cries. For a split second Jess is afraid, too, and Olive grips his arm. Maybe it *is* a Protagon. But the shadow resolves into four or five kids in bathing suits. Beach towels flap from their outstretched arms as they run through the pilings in tight formation. One of them holds up a piece of driftwood with kelp wound around it like a caduceus. Affixed to its top is an old kite. They're all laughing and having fun. The crazy man jerks the Book of Jack from Olive's hands and scrambles away, kicking sand at them. They watch as he melts into the darkness, a shade among deeper shades.

8

# Bernie

Olive lives in a one-story four-plex clad in chestnut brown wood shingles, tikki-style. It sits in what looks like a vacant lot behind a row of bungalows on Paloma Street, a few blocks from the beach. Tall unkempt weeds crowd the porches and obscure its dark windows. A garden has been attempted in their midst, with bulbous tomatoes and green beans in full flower strung along wire, but the effort at reclamation seems futile.

The apartment is gloomy inside, with walls of rough unfinished wood paneling and a coppery shag carpet so old and dirty it feels like sandpaper to touch. Olive's room, one of four set back from the living room and kitchen like quarters in a submarine, gets virtually no natural light. Its one window looks out on a phalanx of bamboo shot through with vines of Virginia creeper.

Jess and Olive lie tangled in the blanket on her futon. It's the only piece of furniture to her name. Clothes are heaped in the corners, and numerous shoes haphazardly clutter the carpet. Nothing adorns the walls except a poster of Marilyn Manson holding his head in his hands.

Jess has pulled off her paisley shirt and now plants her breasts and tattooed stomach with kisses, scenting the almond tang of her skin. His hands slide down her hips. He feels a skittishness in her like a scared animal, but he knows it isn't true: she isn't afraid of anything, or if she is, she'd never admit it to him. It's more adrenalin he feels, coursing, strong, defiant to the point of recklessness. She's good at sex, used to it, knows its paces. But he can tell there's something perfunctory about it for her. Experience betrays her to abstraction already. Maybe because he feels this, or maybe because of his own abstraction, Olive exaggerates the roteness of her gestures, communicating a new irritation. This goes on right through the usual crescendos, muting his final abandon and dissipating its richer intensities. Once he's finished, she turns onto her side and sulks.

"You're not doing it right," she says reproachfully.

He sits up, abashed.

"You're not the only one who wants to get off here, you know. I hate it when guys don't get that."

"I guess I should have...held it, huh?"

This ticks her off even more. "I don't want you to hold it. I want you to do it. Naturally. But it's supposed to happen...," she frowns, "I don't know...at the same time. Or something."

"I guess you have to tell me what you want."

"I want the same thing you do!"

What's that? he wonders.

"I shouldn't have to tell you what I want," she scoffs. "You just know. It's not rocket science. It's not mechanical. There aren't any rules."

He suggests they try again. Against her better judgment, Olive guides him through the labyrinth of female orgasm, at the center of which, and like a kind of minotaur he learns to his young surprise, lies the clitoris. He throws himself into it, or at it, not minding a little sacrifice for the cause. He even discovers new degrees of pleasure in giving pleasure. It excites him to be between her thighs, to feel her ripple out from the mobile tip of his tongue.

But nothing comes easy it turns out, and especially not Olive. He ends up shifting onto his elbow so he can use his finger. All the while she's muttering, "don't stop, don't stop, don't stop." He wonders if it might not be just as well if she took over for him. Why another person for what could be so much better accomplished alone? Just when he feels most irrelevant to the situation, however, she inhales sharply and breaks out in a fierce cry. Pulsations run through her tensed body and she falls quivering into his arms. "Fuck me," she gasps at his ear, and the words thrill him as maybe nothing ever has before. "Right now." He does, with gusto.

A while later they decide to get something to eat. Jess waits for her in the front room. By a window stands a steel cage. In it, a truculent African gray parrot sits on a perch. It eyes Jess with the mistrustful eye of much neglect, squawking miserably. On his approach, the bird cocks its head and poises its beak for attack, in case Jess decides to put his fingers through the bars. He wouldn't think of it. But he retrieves an uneaten sugar snap from the bottom of the cage and tries to feed it. The bird flings it away again, back to where Jess found it.

A girl opens the front door and enters with a bag of groceries in her arm. She's about twenty-five, with long brown hair that falls forward to hide her face.

"Hey," Jess says. "Is this your bird?"

She puts the groceries down on the kitchen counter that opens onto the living room and brushes her hair back. Jess notices one of her eyes is lazy. It looks fixedly off to the side.

"Someone here is keeping it for a friend."

"Does he know how to talk?"

"Never heard him say anything," she says guardedly, as if fighting an urge for flight. Olive appears with a shabby Mohair coat on. Jess can tell at once that she doesn't like her roommate.

"Hey Bernie," she says flatly, then, to Jess, "Let's go, loverboy." They stand there. "Let's go," she urges, annoyed.

The sun is setting as they walk down a driveway past the bungalows. Golden light slants through trees and glows on the stuccoed porches. Two mourning doves teeter on an electrical wire, casting the aspersion of their muted calls on the shadow-bladed street below. Olive's mood has changed.

She's cagey, and she won't look Jess in the eye. Things he says irritate her. He has the feeling she wants to get away, flee back into the seamless anonymity she violated when she spoke to him at the bumper car ride.

"Man, that chick Bernie is something else," she complains as they go. "I've never met anyone so depressing."

"Why is she depressed?"

"Fuck if I know. Or care."

Olive and her other roommates call Bernie the Hermit Crab. She waits tables at the Chowder Room till one in the morning and stays up all night watching old reruns of shows like *Roseanne*, *Home Improvement*, and *Who's the Boss?* During the day she sleeps. When she comes out it might as well be from under a rock. She doesn't have any friends, nobody calls her, and she hardly ever talks. Olive's been trying to figure out how to get rid of her for weeks now.

They walk through the beach flats to the Jack in the Box on PCH. It's almost dark by the time they arrive. The place looks like it's been sacked by a horde of graffiti artists, all working on the theme of Jack the Cat—his tag, cat's heads, cat's paws, caricatures of his face, quotations from the Book. Even the windows get spray paint on them, and everyday an employee has to strip it off with turpentine. Out front, a homeless man with silver eyes talks to himself. He wears a white flat-brimmed straw hat and reminds Jess of Vincent Van Gogh in the south of France. "Holy holy holy holy holy holy holy is the Lord of Hosts," he says quietly. "Holy holy holy holy holy holy holy holy fucking shit…"

Olive strides through the door ignoring him, or used to him. At the counter, she calls out her order of a Spicy Chicken Sandwich Special to a Mexican girl. Jess gets the same. As they wait, he looks around the restaurant and observes other homeless men seated at tables, one with his belongings squeezing out of a torn plastic garbage bag, another with grimy face reciting facts from an old World Almanac, still another glaring with fierce interest at the fluorescent lamp above his head. In fact, except for him and Olive, every customer in the restaurant is crazy.

He asks if she notices this once they've sat down.

"I guess so," she says, munching her food.

"Why do they come here?"

"It's not hard to figure out, Einstein. You get fries and a burger for four bucks. It's warm, and there's a bathroom with running water. This is probably where I'd be nights, if I were on the street."

A white flash in the window attracts her attention, and she twists around to follow an old Chevrolet with fish-tail fins into the parking lot. Soon two unusual guys come through the door. One has his hair in a greasy pompadour that he's in the process of combing back from an already thinning hairline. He wears a T-shirt with RANCID stenciled on the front and pants with turned up cuffs. The other looks like a leprechaun, with dyed rust-colored hair, green eyes, masses of freckles on his flushed cheeks, and a silver loop in his ear.

"Hey Mose!" cries Olive, waving at them.

"Fuckin' A, Mr. Naked," says the first guy to his friend. "If it ain't Olive, the rockabilly bitch."

"No way, dude," she drawls. "Now I'm a hippie 'ho."

"You know what's the difference between a bitch and a 'ho, don't you?" says the guy Mose calls Mr. Naked.

"What?"

"A 'ho fucks everybody. A bitch fucks everybody but you."

"Know a lot of bitches, huh?" cracks Olive.

"I know you," he shoots back.

"What are you two up to?" she asks with a laugh.

"Headed for the Ace of Hearts," says Mose. "After we chow down."

"Who's playing?"

"What does it matter...," Mose says, and for Olive this is her cue to chime in on their old mantra: "*So long as it rocks!*"

Fifteen minutes later, Jess finds himself seated in the back of the Chevy with Mose's friend, tagging along to a club on Del Mar Street.

"Why does he call you Mr. Naked?" asks Jess.

"That's my name."

"Naked?"

"Buck Naked. You can call me Buck."

"Wasn't that a band or something?"

"Buck Naked and the Bare Bottom Boys," interjects Mose.

"That was before I died," says Buck. "Up in 'Frisco. This nut killed me because I chased his pigeons away one night in a park." He feigns a world-weary sigh and looks off. "Long time ago now."

As it turns out, tonight is '60s night at the Ace of Hearts, and the featured band is a bunch of skinny androgynous guys with long hair playing covers of dreamy songs by the Yardbirds and Buffalo Springfield. The keyboardist is jamming on his Hammond organ, and the lead singer has his microphone crammed to his lips like a harmonica, crooning serenely into the p.a. system.

The club is thronged with enthusiasts of the decade, each dressed variously in bushy sideburns, mop wigs, white plastic belts with huge buckles, particolored shirts, and boots with square toes. Even the cocktail waitresses and bartenders have gotten into the act. The effect is so complete Jess feels transported back to the year 1968. Everything is exactly as it was then. He hasn't even been born yet.

They snag a red leather booth in the back of the club and are soon joined by more compadres. About eight people end up crammed together around the Formica table, drinking beers and goofing around. Olive is in her element now, sarcastically commiserating over the music to a girl with pageboy bangs and dark purple lipstick about the hardships of keeping up her image. Their voices are sharp as they mime the loose shoulders, fluttering eyelids, and cocked heads of flighty socialites.

"I'm so tired of bad hair days," drawls Olive.

"I never have a bad hair day," replies her friend, "because I use the three-step Butylidene Treatment Plan, with special follicle implants made of silicon. It seals and smooths my hair, without build-up. Plus it takes the frizz out of the curl and increases shine!"

They gaze hilariously into each other's eyes, like lesbians in love, peck each other on the lips and snort in crude pleasure at their odd parody, waving cigarettes in the air. Mose is running a metal tine back and forth through the hole pierced in the cartilage between his nostrils, like a magician, for the enjoyment of a guy who resembles one of those reptiles that fan out their faces in times of danger. Directly across from Jess, a girl with light gray eyes and a long face reminds him of some lean, half-starved stray kitten. Her eyes flare and bulge with strange regularity. She seems sore about something, for she sits sullenly in a world of her own, staring at the smoke that coils above the table.

"It sucks, man," says a girl next to him. She follows this with a loud belch. He turns to take in a mohawk of orange-red spikes and a face so thick with makeup it looks as if swatches of clay had been flung at it by a sculptor.

"What sucks?" Jess asks.

"This scene. I hate the Sixties. Anything before the Dead Kennedys is for geezers."

He nods. Not much more to say about that. "Do you always dress this way?"

"No," she says. "I was just an extra at a film shoot up in LA. That's my job. Whenever they need a punk rocker, they call on me."

Jess falls silent. He feels uncomfortable. Scenes like this one make him want to be alone, to make a feeling he has anyway real. He hates this about himself. He wishes he could take part in the repartee, the joshing and skylarking. He likes the people around him well enough. They show a willingness to accept him into their circle, too. Buck and Mose are curious to find out he's in the Navy. They've been thinking of enlisting, but somehow they keep putting it off. He doesn't know what to tell them about that, and he's glad when they don't press him on it. Conversation swerves off into other topics, their friend's Sherlock Holmes pipe, the scummy gutter punk Mose used to date, how they're going to get so ripped tonight it's not even funny.

The band finishes a set and takes a break. The lead singer ambles up to the table. He has dirty blonde hair that curves like question marks around a sensitive oval face, and he speaks in a voice so soft you can barely hear it. Everything about him says "soulful."

"Hi Olive," he sighs.

"That was so rad, Kip," she says, and everyone around the booth agrees.

"We got a gig in Anaheim next Saturday," he says. "We open for The Cannabinoids. We're doing *Bitch's Brew*."

"Cool, dude," says Mose.

"Still got that Harley?" inquires Olive.

"Love to give you a ride sometime," he says, emoting heavily.

So would Olive, Jess observes. A jealous squall lashes through his heart. There will be more as the evening progresses, but they never manage to coalesce in storm. They drain into the watershed of a strange self-consciousness and leave no trace, only the promise of more luxuriant growth in some future springtime. It pains him that Kip would know how to make Olive come, but then what right has he to care? He has no history here. He hasn't put down any stakes, any roots. He's just a sailor passing through, even if that's not all he is right now either. His allegiance is still to things that move. Salute the captain on the quarterdeck, salute the flag over the fantail—those are the two nations he belongs to.

They drink beers through another set. After the band clears out, the club metamorphoses into a disco with pulsing strobe lights, old movies projected onto the walls, and go-go girls dancing in suspended cages. A DJ spins a mix of Mersey sound, classic rock'n'roll, Mod, and Glam-rock over techno beats. Pretty soon the club is thumping. The booth has been vacated for the dance floor, and only Jess and the girl who resembles a half-starved kitten remain behind. She's unhappy at the wallflower status she shares with him yet stubbornly set against doing anything about it. They've both decided that there can be no solidarity between them.

Presently he gets up and wanders through the club. He walks past the coat-check girl in her little booth, stops to watch the games of pool, and heads upstairs to a tepid S-n-M scene on the mezzanine. A fat girl in a rig of complicated black leather straps, silver studs, and fishnet tights hangs by her wrists from manacles while a muscular bald man whips her back. A midget with big boobs props her high-heeled foot on a chair, bends over and lets another woman stroke her crotch with a peacock feather.

Jess, rapidly losing interest, turns to wedge himself into a spot at the rail. From there he can look out over the whole club. Down on the dance floor, Olive and Kip are mesmerizing each other with their snakey moves. He starts thinking maybe this isn't so much fun anymore. Just then Mose and Buck appear, looking for some private place to lay down a few lines of cocaine they just scored. They tried the bathroom but the club keeps a monitor in there, and it's too dark on the mezzanine.

They reconnoiter with their friends at the booth on how to solve this problem. They could go to the car, or they could be bold and just do it on the Formica table. A flushed and sweaty Olive suggests they walk over to her place, only a few blocks away, and come back. This appeals to everyone, so Jess follows Mose, Buck, Olive, and Kip out to Del Mar Street.

The sidewalks are crowded and the bars are full. The new movie complex with its massive neon marquee is bustling. Clumps of people gather around street entertainers: a tap-dancing duo, a 12-year-old blues guitar phenom from Taiwan, an old man in suspenders who plays musical saw. The gold lamé man stands stone still on his pedestal. On a bench outside an art gallery sit two old ladies cast in bronze, their hands gesticulating, their expressions serious, their mouths contorted around the syllables of an animated discussion. Jess sees a man with a Charlie McCarthy doll seated on a milk crate doing his routine, and he wonders if it's the same duo who got high with Jack the Cat. The boardwalk hums in the background, as omnipresent as a beached sea monster.

An impromptu party ensues in Olive's living room, to the dismay of the parrot, who screeches at all comers. The ritual of snorting cocaine unfolds around the coffee table, with Mose as high priest. Olive and Kip lie slumped together on the sofa, shoulders and knees grazing. They speak of people they know, old high school scandals, a life in common. It's as if Jess has ceased to exist. Another of those jealous squalls carries him away to the bathroom, right before his turn comes with the communal straw. He walks down the hallway and hears the sound of a television come from one of the bedrooms. That must be Bernie watching her reruns. Through the wall in the bathroom he can even tell what show it is: *Mr. Belvedere.* Oh brother. It's all so sad. But then again, what does he know? Maybe it's not sad. Maybe he's the sad one. That's the only honest thing to say, even if it hardly seems more honest to stop short of sympathy like that.

At hand is a return exodus to the Ace of Hearts. Jess meets Olive at the entrance just as Kip slips outside. "Are you coming?" she asks a little sheepishly. He can tell she doesn't want him to.

"I think I'll be heading home," he says. "My uncle expects me."

"Can't keep daddy-o waiting!"

Mose pushes her out the door and calls on him to follow after. Jess stands there until he can't hear them in the driveway anymore and is about to leave. On a whim he goes back down the hall to knock on Bernie's door. She opens it and stares, scratching her cheek. The dark moody room behind her is as unkempt as she is, cluttered with her things. Her hair sticks out in all directions as if she's been sleeping. She wears flannel pajamas with little Winnie the Poohs on it. That lazy eye keeps watch on the hallway behind as she waits for him to say something.

"Hey," he stammers.

"Hey."

"I'm Jess. I didn't say, earlier..."

"I'm Bernie."

"Isn't that a guy's name?" he asks conversationally.

"Isn't Jess a girl's name?"

That takes him aback. "I guess so."

"Mine's short for Bernadette."

"Oh." He rubs his jaw. "What are you up to?"

"Aren't you going with the others?" she asks.

"No. I don't feel like it." She slowly withdraws, letting the door swing open behind her. "Can I come in?"

"I'm not sure."

"It's all right," he says. "I promise I'm not a serial killer."

She lays on the bed and fixes her gaze on the television screen, wary but interested enough, too, it seems. He stands by the door, as there isn't any place for him to sit. She gathers her quilt till it covers her up to her chin.

"Staying home tonight, huh?"

There's a commercial on for some drug that cures male impotence. A man smiles into his wife's face while a rapid-fire voice lists all the ailments you might get if you take it. Bernie turns the volume down with her remote control. "Yeah."

"Anything on?"

"No. Same old thing."

"You watch a lot of TV?"

This makes her suspicious. "How do you know?"

He hesitates before saying, "Olive told me."

"Olive," she echoes, and there is a distinct plaintive intonation in her voice.

"I was wondering why you do it, that's all," he says with a candor that disarms her a little.

She picks pill balls off the quilt and forms a pile with them. "What's it to you?"

"It just seems like a strange thing to do."

"No stranger than anything else."

"You don't have to answer if you don't want to."

She sticks her finger in her ear and wiggles it. "I suppose I don't see the point of going out."

"It's fun sometimes, isn't it?"

"Not for me."

"Why not?"

"You really want to know?"

"Yeah."

He sees her wondering herself what the answer might be and guesses she hasn't ever been asked quite this directly before. But she tries to sort one out.

"I stay in because people are mean," she says finally. "They hurt you without thinking twice about it, just because they can, and I get tired of that."

Right away she doesn't like how this sounds. "It's more that people are fake," she says, trying another tack. "They're always pretending to be something they're not, and I hate that. I hate how impersonal it is. I hate how random and empty it makes me feel."

The silence that follows this disclosure is heightened, as if the room has been magnetized and hums in a force field. The moment seems still all of a sudden, like it might in eternity, Jess thinks, and he feels, for the first time maybe, how quietly a person can lose himself in the world.

"Is everybody fake?"

"Pretty much."

"Am I?" he asks.

"You might be. I don't know yet." Jess surprises her with a crestfallen look. "I'm just being honest."

"No, I understand. That's what I wanted. I could kind of sense that about you. And I was thinking, just now, how it isn't possible to be honest anymore. Maybe it never has been."

"I think it is."

"You do?"

"It's just that, when you are, nobody likes it."

"Yeah," he nods. "Why is that?"

"Nobody wants to admit they're fake."

He nods again. "Would it be any different, if you did admit it?"

"Sure," she says. "There's something that's not fake, too. You can step out of it, see it for what it is."

Her words stir a wild hope in Jess's heart. They have him wanting to say things he's never been able to say before, in a language more like song, which reveals how random and empty he, too, feels.

What comes out is different. "I'm in the Navy," he tells her. "I got into some trouble. They gave me this three-day pass, only they weren't supposed to, because I was supposed to be somewhere else the same day. I took it anyway. Now I'm...AWOL, kind of. And I don't want to go back. I don't want to do it anymore."

This couldn't have been further from heartfelt song. He wonders if he'll ever be able to express himself that way, or if anyone could. Maybe thinking anyone could was the real mistake. Maybe life was made up only of accumulated failures like this one, little lost opportunities to connect that never have the traction they need, and the trick is to accept this, to stop trying for honesty. A wan smile plays into his face, and even if Bernie doesn't quite understand what he's feeling, she recognizes in it a familiar chill disappointment.

"I have a cousin who ran away from the Army," she says. "He hitchhiked from Fort Irwin in the Mojave Desert all the way to Texas. He made it to Dallas and lived there for about six months. But they caught up with him in the end, and he spent two years in prison. Leavenworth. He was never the same after that."

Jess, of course, has been trying his best not to think of what would happen if he goes back to North Island tomorrow, let alone if he doesn't. Maybe they would stop at a reprimand and a reassignment, since he has the chit to show them and can just play dumb. People miss their ships all the time. But it would be pretty craven of him to count on this. He really didn't want to go back. Leaving the base yesterday was as close to a true decision as he's ever gotten, and he wants to respect that. He wants to face the challenge of a freedom for which he's had little preparation and maybe less talent, but which presented itself as never before when he turned around on that pier.

He can see, though, that he won't be able to do it. There seems no way to do it. The options all collapse in on one another: taking a stand and running away, true decision and denial, spirit and dread. He can't sort them into any freedom worth the name.

"What are you going to do?" Bernie asks him.

He presses his lips together. "I don't know."

She stares, her eyes brightening with a cold light that might be the blue reflection of the television. "Have you ever felt like you don't want to live anymore?" she asks then, her voice without inflection as if spellbound. "Like if you could do it, get rid of yourself, you would?"

He wonders how close she's come to so desperate a resolve. Have there been for her moments of that much despair in this room, seeking a past, a place, a sense of permanence from what was only ever as solid as pixelated images on a screen? But no, he's never felt that way. "I've only felt I couldn't do it," he says, "even if I wanted to. I can't *not* live. I'm stuck with myself."

There's no escape, he realizes. No way out that's not just another way in, like a revolving door. And this, paradoxically enough, means there's only escape, only a desire for something else delivering people all over again to the same old thing, turning on its own axis. That's why Bernie hides in here. That's why even despair feels dishonest. It turns on itself, or against itself; it despairs of despair itself, if that makes any sense. Putting it like this prompts a shift, anyway, a change into another state that Jess can almost say is beautiful despite its harsh necessity, as beautiful as Bernie's lazy eye or the blue flicker of television light flung against the rough wood paneling above her bed or his own ghostly impulse to talk to her. Life really is random and empty. It has no consistency or even coherence, no other than this turning or this redoubling structure. It's crazy, in a word. And yet, just because it's crazy he supposes, that's what has to be affirmed about it. One has to live not against the craziness but from it, or with it, on the strength of it even, for the chance at novelty in repetition, like a boy running in a flipbook. Jess wonders if he has that in him, given his nature and everything he's been through lately, but the idea of trying does have its appeal, its draw in the heart. He can say that. It hints at a reason for faith he's never quite considered before.

"Do you play Scrabble?" Bernie asks.

"What?" He didn't hear.

"Scrabble."

"Oh."

"I have a board. Do you want to play?"

"Sure."

Bernie pulls the box down from the top shelf of her closet and makes a space on the bed, smoothing out the quilt. She opens the board and parses the letters, her head bent so her hair falls forward to cover her face. Jess joins her, feeling his moment of insight, if that's what it was, fade away again, back into the crazy world. He sorts his letters on the wooden placeholder she gives him, looking for combinations, for words he doesn't know how to form yet, and pretty soon they are deep in their game.

9

# Milo's Day

On the boardwalk, Milo watches a guy rotate in a contraption made of hooped steel. The guy grins and blushes red as the sudden shifts in direction jerk his body this way and that in its velcro straightjacket. Round and round, Milo thinks from his place in the crowd, movement subjected to a rigid stasis. People going nowhere fast. It seems appropriate in its futility. What Milo doesn't understand is why people like it. Candy, gravity, and hormones! he hears himself saying. Okay, okay. But why that would be enough, and why people would settle for the formula of their own human nature implied in its holy trifecta, still baffles him.

It didn't used to be true. In the old days people wanted to understand how rigged and framed things were. They tried to get out of the system, to challenge the status quo. They even had fun doing it. Nowadays it's just the opposite. There's no feeling for resistance. No one wants to rebel.

Moving on, Milo recalls the little formative moments of his own decision to hate authority for as long as he lives: his girlfriend Judy, just out of juvenile hall, wearing knee-length suede boots that she'd bought for a buck at a thrift store in Orange; Bob Dylan's "Subterranean Homesick Blues"; Lenny Bruce's brassy stuck-up voice on the radio; the first time the cops stopped him just because he had long hair; dropping acid at Balboa Week up in Newport; the light shows at Harmony Park; and above all, the bikers with long leather coats he saw when he was thirteen outside a Clifton's Cafeteria on Harbor Boulevard, roaring down the road with their cut-outs open. He knew then that, no matter what happened to him later on, the sound of those cut-outs would run through his life like a theme song. After that, there was no turning back: Milo was a renegade.

The boardwalk, as if charged with electric current, tingles beneath his feet, making his legs go slowly numb. He takes this as a sign that he's had enough of the board-walk for one day, and he heads for a secret exit he knows behind the Logjammer millpond. But on the way he passes the new dinosaur ride and remembers he'd made a few large papier-mâché mushrooms for Special Effects that ended up in there, so he decides to take a look at them before he goes. He pays for a ticket, waits through the line, and sits in the car next to a six-year-old girl.

"Where's your kid?" she asks, smart as a whip. Milo likes her at once.

"I don't have a kid. I'm the kid."

The car rolls on in to a dinosaur cave, and they start passing by brontosauruses up to their shoulders in water, flying pterodactyls, a rampaging Tyrannosaurus rex. Milo catches sight of his mushrooms, orange with yellow spots, on a green bank, and he flushes with pride. Otherwise, he's not impressed. He can see wire mesh emerge from the hairy rump of a stegosaurus, and one wing on a pterodactyl looks like a blown-out spinnaker. Tiny lights bob from fishing wire and are supposed to be fireflies, but they just look like lights hanging from fishing wire. And, to top it all off, he sees a bunch of hairy Neanderthals crouching around a campfire. Only Neanderthals, he silently laments, would put Neanderthals with dinosaurs.

Two kids in the front seat of the car lean toward each other and comment on how much the ride reminds them of *Jurassic Park*. Milo, appalled, turns to the little girl beside him and finds, to his relief, that she's frowning right back at him.

"*Jurassic Park*'s about one billion times better," she tells him under her breath. "They don't know what they're talking about."

He hasn't even seen *Jurassic Park*, but he can tell she's a little lady of discernment, and after his own heart. It's obvious there's no magic here. It requires imagination and care to make you feel like you're right in the middle of a magic world. Neither went into this ride.

Once outside he finds the secret entrance, a path threading the steel beam foundation of the millpond where log boats float to the exit platform. From there he slides down a short dirt slope and slips through a gap between two oleander bushes onto the street, not far from where they'd left the bikes. He leaves Jess's behind, making a mental note to himself to collect it later, and sets off on his own, out of the boardwalk's hulking shadow. He rides along an embankment that stretches as far as the wharf, flinging up his eyes to take in the row of skinny palm trees as they sway gently against the blue sky. The sunny day persuades him, with the air hissing past his neck, to stay outside with the madding crowds a while longer. Let's see what East Brother's up to, he says to himself.

On the other side of the wharf is the beachfront esplanade, backed by a row of old hotels in Spanish Mission and Craftsman styles. Abalone shells glitter brilliantly in the concrete, and silver posts, staggered at twenty-foot intervals, uphold blue ship's lamps. Lucy used to be the person who turned off the lights back when the promenade was a wood-plank boardwalk, and before that on the old pier, long since gone. She had to walk down the hill every night, carrying a small stepladder with her so she could turn the knobs on the carbide lamps. Later, when they converted to electricity, she had to set the timer so the lights went off at ten o'clock. If the timer didn't work, she had to take her stepladder all the way down again and turn each one off by hand.

He runs into a woman he knows, Cathy, and slows down to chat. She's petite and blonde, nice in a vague sort of way, the old girlfriend of someone he used to know. They went to the same parties in their younger days. They never had much in common, but they also never had much reason to dislike each other, so these accidental run-ins are pleasant enough.

He rides beside her, slowing the bike down to a snail's pace. She tells him about the clothes store for children she opened with her sister in a mini-mall on PCH, how bad business has been, and how she's not sure it's going to last much longer. She's married now to a guy named Steve, a guitarist who sells life insurance on the side. Milo guesses he's an insurance salesman who plays guitar on the side, but he doesn't say anything.

"You sure are going slow on that bike," she observes. "You're hardly moving at all. How do you keep balanced like that?"

Milo beams. He's always been proud of his prowess on a bike. "Easy," he says. "You just have to stay real still and poised, like you were a tightrope walker." The handlebars wobble a little, and he taps the pedals for momentum.

At Calle San Juan Cathy says goodbye and turns off. He rides hard to the end of the esplanade and rumbles down a wood platform that stretches over the sand almost to the water's edge. The beach terminates at the foot of West Cliff underneath the cantilevers of the

Albatross Restaurant, where old movie stars used to come back in the '40s. The perpendicular curve of the bluff and rocky irregularities in the ocean bottom make for an unusual confluence of waves. Wedges rear up in spikes fifteen feet high sometimes, lifting you into the air and grinding you back down into the sand. But they also afford crazy possibilities for boogie boarders and body surfers. It was always Milo's favorite spot for that. He lays his bike by the edge of the platform and sits at the shoreline. The wedge is out about twenty yards. People bob in its vicinity, waiting for one of those weird diagonal waves or a chance at sudden apotheosis.

The waves are crisp and shapely nearer the beach. He fixes his attention on one kid who methodically works this more modest precinct almost by himself. Milo approves. There are two kinds of people in the world on his account: those who swim out beyond the surf line and those who stay close to shore. Those who like to brave the sublime mysteries of the open sea and flirt recklessly with disaster, and those who prefer the intimate pressures and dynamics of the water's edge.

The kid wears a wetsuit, but through it Milo can tell he's a little overweight and that makes him self-conscious and a loner. He's a nice kid with a crewcut who hasn't learned who to hate yet. And he also knows how to feel his way with the sea, skillfully maneuvering himself into position on the sheer face of the wave with his board and flipper. Sometimes he even slips into a tube.

When he does, Milo sees him crane his neck and open his eyes wide on that brief vision of crystal paradise.

"You're a pretty good boogie boarder," he tells him when he hauls himself out. The kid blushes and says nothing, but Milo can see he appreciates the compliment. In fact, he'll probably remember it for a long time, think of it when other people make him feel stupid or clumsy, and rely on it when the whole world is saying he should grow up and get a job. Milo used to receive similar compliments. He was a good fisherman, for instance. When he'd go out to the end of the wharf to fish, people used to tell him he had the right touch with a rod. Once he caught a 62-pound sea bass using a homemade trout pole with a 15-pound test line, and as far as he knows people still talk about that around town.

But recognition like this has been the exception, not the rule. No one's ever really given Milo the encouragement he needed. When he was a kid his folks never told him the whale box he made was cool or the drawing he did was interesting. It wasn't even personal or mean. They stared back at him when he needed support not because they didn't care but because they couldn't; it was blockage, incapacity, that met him in their earnest faces, something nobody could do anything about even if they wanted to. It was like cows, he thinks, the way they look chewing cud. He's wracked his brain trying to figure that blank look out, especially in his dad, dead these past ten years now. It wasn't stupidity, and yet it wasn't not stupidity either.

His dad was a smart guy. He knew a lot of things, like how to put new bushings in a car's water pump, or pack in the fairings, or braze its frame back together again. But he drove that car every day for forty years to his job at a television repair shop and never gave it a second thought. That still blows Milo's mind.

He gets back on his bike and makes his way up to West Cliff Drive. It curves along the bluffs with a view to the wharf and boardwalk beyond. Eventually it hits a stone castle built long ago by an eccentric millionaire. The castle, with a turret on each corner, stands in a headland demesne of cypress trees and airy eucalyptuses fallen into blight. Next to that, on a finger of slowly eroding earth thrust out to sea, stands the lighthouse, a small whitewashed structure surmounted by its massive revolving light. There hasn't been a lighthouse keeper since the facility was automated in 1964, and the building has lately been converted into a museum devoted to the history of an arts festival, the Masquerade of the Gods. In 1910, a cohort of landscape painters were shut out from the Pageant of the Masters in Laguna Beach, so they started their own rival festival in East Brother. Like the Pageant it boasted a parade, lifesized tableaux of biblical scenes, and art shows, but on a smaller scale and with a more down-to-earth style. In recent years the Masquerade of the Gods languished and finally petered out, but its heyday has been commemorated in the museum with photographs, posters, relics, and oldtimers' anecdotes that you can listen to on audio headsets.

Milo pedals along the cliffside walkway to the grassy sward surrounding the lighthouse. He stops by a bronze statue of a heroic surfer, board in hand, feet firmly planted, chest out, eyebeam far, and looks down on the swaying water. Arms of brown kelp move fitfully in the green depths, beckoning or warning off he can't tell which. In one spot, rolling beads of water hint at a rock ledge just beneath the surface. Pelicans with outstretched wings descend in a row, adjusting themselves here and there to the modulations of the water. In a notch of the cliff just beneath, Milo glimpses a couple of huddled cormorants, awaiting a whim to depart.

He turns to face the lighthouse. Numerous gourd-shaped nests crowd under its eaves, and swallows dart in and out of the black round holes, hunting for insects to give their chicks. The air is swarming with them. Milo walks his bike over to look for dead chicks on the ground beneath. There are usually a few to be found, when it comes time to learn how to fly. On the way he passes an old man seated at a bench. He has a grave old-world demeanor, with a craggy tanned face and dark brown eyes, sad almost to the point of caricature. He wears a blue reefer jacket with gilt buttons, a bright scarlet red handkerchief in his breast pocket, a primly knotted and bowed cravat at his throat, and a matching blue cap. Thin wrists and hands lay crossed upon the bulbous knob of a walking stick, propped in front of him. He, too, is looking at the swallows.

"Fascinating, huh?" says Milo, pausing to take in the scene. "You can watch them for hours."

The old man sighs. "Have you ever noticed that the nests resemble faces?" he asks. "Tortured faces?" He has a heavy accent.

Milo squints at them again. "No, I haven't. But now that you mention it, I see what you mean."

"They're faces in hell," continues the old man, in a kind of trance, "their blank mouths howling wordless torments."

"They don't have eyes, either. Their faces are melted or something. Maybe it's all that fire in hell," he adds with a smirk.

This shakes the old man from his somber mood. In a more affable tone he says, "They remind me of Goya's madhouses."

Milo's impressed. He doesn't know anything about Goya's madhouses, but he remembers looking at his *Disasters of War* etchings in a book: peasants executed by frenzied firing squads, priests impaled on tree branches, monsters gorging on human flesh, cats with griffin's wings, soldiers with demon leers running people through with swords, weird shit. "You must be an artist," he says.

The old man cocks a derisive eye at him. "What's that?"

"Somebody who paints pictures."

He smiles. "I guess I'm an artist, then."

"You also gotta get paid," Milo says, unsure of himself all of a sudden. "Maybe it isn't enough to have a bunch of rolled up paintings in your garage."

"By that august standard, too, I'm an artist."

"What do you paint?"

"Zurbaráns," the man says.

"Zurbaráns?"

He nods.

Milo arches a brow, rubs his cheeks, and puckers. After a few seconds he says, "I don't understand."

"I paint exactly as Francisco de Zurbarán did four hundred years ago. In fact, if you ensure the authenticity of the canvas and use the same pigments, there is absolutely no way to tell the difference."

"No kidding? That's amazing."

His name is Gaspar Melchor Osorio de Zuniga, and he's an orphan from Extremadura, a province of western Spain. As he goes on to tell Milo in some detail, his unknown parents had abandoned him as an infant on the doorstep of a Catholic orphanage, run by dour nuns who lacked all warmth and sympathy. He grew up resented for his sensitive nature, spurned in his interests and encouraged only in what he despised. His salvation was Zurbarán, also from Extremadura, whose work he first saw as a boy in books he chanced upon in a public library. He would pour over them on the rare occasions the nuns allowed him to spend an afternoon there, and afterward, at the orphanage, he would retreat to his bunk and treasure the images in his mind's eye for hours on end.

When he was twelve, he saw his first real Zurbarán in a museum. It depicted the martyred Saint Serapion, bound hands raised in quasi-crucifixion, canted head resting in his cape, eyes closed on infinite sorrow. The soft swirls of paint shading the saint's bruised and battered brow moved Gaspar to tears. The deep shadows in the chiseled folds of white cloth that hung from his shoulders, rendered in broad strokes against a backdrop of impenetrable emptiness, struck him as miraculous. He heard a voice in his head, more intimate than his own, speak to him of a passion so profound, yet so buried, that only absolute sacrifice could bring it out. A sense of destiny seized him. He would be an artist like Zurbarán.

He had no training and no direction, so he had to teach himself the techniques of drawing and painting. But they came easily to him, and before long he was reproducing Zurbaráns from the library books with an unnerving accuracy. At seventeen the nuns sent him away to a school of mines and engineering in Seville, where he neglected his studies in art classes he took at night. His teachers noticed his preternatural skill and encouraged him to develop his own style. Yet whenever he tried something else, the results were cold and lifeless. He felt hobbled by their freedom and debased by their imagination. After many failures he could only conclude that his teachers didn't understand. They lacked the sensibility to recognize true talent. Gaspar had a style, and it was Zurbarán's. Everything else was philistine.

After graduating from the school of mines, he moved to Madrid and worked as a station operator in the metro. Every spare moment he spent at museums, devouring Zurbarán line by line, hue by hue, brushstroke by brushstroke. At night he set out with single-minded dedication to replicate what he'd seen as perfectly as he could. Exhaustion and sleeplessness led to a strange participation in the mind of the painter. So far inside his eye and touch did he go that he lost any sense of the difference between them. He was Zurbarán in his tiny studio off the Dos de Mayo Square, feverishly at work in the dead of night. What Zurbarán thought, he thought, too; what Zurbarán could not deny himself, in like manner neither could he. Over the years this almost diabolical possession became second nature, making him so bold in his work that he graduated from replicas to original canvasses that matched Zurbarán's genius in every tint, shade, mark, speck, and antiqued patina.

He had few illusions about how the world would receive his masterpieces, yet he had the same desire for recognition as anyone who devotes himself to patient labor and suffers for his creations. For a long time he considered the best way to present his work to the public, in such a light that its brilliance would be allowed to shine. In the end, he chose to reveal his secret to an auction dealer with a special interest in the Baroque. Gaspar had heard him give a lecture at the Prado, detecting a dark passion like his own and a chance at mutual understanding. He arrived one day at the dealer's office with a framed painting of a man playing a lute by candlelight, wrapped in linen. He presented himself as a go-between for a reclusive eccentric who preferred to remain anonymous, and was about to embellish this lie further when the dealer, drawing aside the linen to examine the painting, gasped, "A Zurbarán!"

Gaspar stammered out his crucial qualification, but it went unheard. The dealer seized the painting in both hands and stared at the raking light, the foreshortened space, the almost narcotic austerity of its geometric design. He promptly called scholars, collectors, and traders from all over Europe, and a day later they met in Madrid to sequester themselves with the find. Hours after they emerged in a state of frantic excitement to confirm the initial pronouncement.

News spread fast that a lost Zurbarán had been discovered by an unknown patron, and Gaspar, swept up in forces that brooked no resistance, found himself a month after that in the audience at Christie's as his painting sold for $25,000,000.

Milo is by now seated on the bench, bike flat on the ground, listening with bated breath to the old man's story. Of course, things changed dramatically for him from that time on. He went from being a nobody, a crazy enigmatic loner frittering his life away in weird obsession, to a debonair citizen of the world. He lived in Paris, New York, Mallorca, the Alps, Greek islands. He furnished another fake original from the same mysterious patron, which sold for twice the figure of the first. For the next decade he unveiled one a year, claiming they came from a cache of paintings long thought lost at sea on a voyage to Peru in 1653. By the end Gaspar was worth $300,000,000.

He was much sought after. His natural but much thwarted sensitivity had at last found its aristocratic bloom. He developed refined opinions about art and fashion, and crown-princes considered him a prize at elegant soirees. Movie stars threw themselves at him. Some he gratified, and some he spurned without a quiver of regret. He counted among his friends heiresses, heads of state, Nobel-prize-winning novelists, and famous film directors. Nothing was denied him. Everything was possible.

But then it all came crashing down. The one flaw in his gem-like world was that he could never take credit for his work. He was always the suave, ironic connoisseur, never the virile, demiurgic artist. To others, he knew everything about Zurbarán except his genius; he longed to reveal to them just how much he knew about that, too. The confession occasionally formed itself on his lips, its first syllables stumbling out of his mouth, and only fright or luck prevented him from destroying himself. What finally did him in was greed. A shady art dealer mentioned a Hungarian count interested in procuring a known Zurbarán drawing that Gaspar had copied to perfection. In a moment of weakness he sold it to the dealer, and when it was discovered, the dealer betrayed him. Gaspar was exposed as a forger and brought before a courtroom in Paris, where he tearfully admitted to his singular talent and even more singular deception.

The scandal rocked the art world. It spread chaos among the Brahmin classes of experts and aficionados, some of whom refused to believe him, some of whom demanded his head in a basket. Stock markets dipped in fear of the magnitude of his fraud, and only an embarrassed desire on the part of the art world to mute the affair in the media kept him from a public lynching. He spent ten years in the Santé prison for his crimes and upon his release discovered he was still not free, since the authorities found it prudent to keep him, and his unique abilities, under constant surveillance. He left Europe for America.

"I ended up here in East Brother," he says. "I decided to lead an honest life. I was talented, after all. I knew how to paint! I had felt more than any man has a right to feel and still survive. Why could I not bring forth the extremes of despair and bliss I had experienced as an orphan multi-millionaire? So I decided to be a humble painter named Gaspar Melchor Osorio de Zuniga. I would ply my trade, sign my name with honor to my own work, and let it stand or fall on its merits."

"Did you?" says Milo with trepidation.

Sorrow steals over the old man's face. "I tried, I really tried. I painted flowers in vaporous sea-green vases, irises, grape hyacinths, false indigo, and cornflowers. I painted sunsets, skies with clouds in them and skies without clouds. I painted the sea, leaping swordfish of gold-marbled sapphire, turquoise anemones clustered in ocher-warmed aquamarine coves. I made a modest living selling them to tourists through the galleries here: fifty dollars without frames, or seventy-five with—"

"Then you're an artist!" cries Milo. "You're doing exactly what you want to do: making your money on art, the honest way. That's a lot to be proud of!"

Gaspar shakes his head. "No," he says. "They were pretty, but they weren't art. The wells of my genius had run dry. I was just a two-bit hack. None of it mattered because it didn't come from the heart." His eyes moisten. "Because what I really wanted to do, what burned in me like a star in celestial wastes, what flung me to heights of rapture, moved me beyond words and shook the very foundations of my soul, was to paint, in spotlit highlights, the saints, ecstatic monks, and angelic messengers of Francisco de Zurbarán."

This last is spoken in hushed tones as if it were a confidence, not meant to be published abroad. Milo is beginning to suspect the old guy might be senile.

"So what did you do?" he asks.

"I began to paint them again. In the strictest secrecy. I accepted my fate and devoted myself to the one thing I was meant to do, despite the censure of my peers and the outrage of the civilized world." He glances rapidly across both shoulders. He leans in and adds *sotto voce*, "I now have dozens of luminous, incomparably perfect, incontestably original Zurbarán masterpieces."

After a pregnant silence, disturbed only by the chirps of slashing swallows, Milo asks, "Where are they?"

"I keep them rolled up in my garage."

Gaspar then alludes to the likely presence of Interpol agents in the vicinity, there to ensure that he does not revert to his former pastime or consort with undesirables who might wish to exploit him for gain. A twinging fear in Milo throws Gaspar's story into the light of possible apocrypha. What should he believe? That in some old guy's East Brother garage is a cache of fake paintings worth about a billion dollars? He almost prefers that to the alternative, which is that he's been having a serious conversation with a madman for half an hour now. But either way, Milo feels a drift in the points of reference on which he normally relies for his bearings, and he isn't sure he likes the confusion or what it bodes for him. He figures it might be time to move on.

He remounts his bike, says so long to Gaspar, and leaves him to the swallows and his melancholy. As he rides off his thoughts change into a darker key. He wonders what his passion is, his holy grail, the inmost terminus of his deepest rapture? What is it that burns in him like a star in celestial wastes? He has no answer and never has had one when it comes down to it, sad to say. He's never been able to take himself that seriously. Dispossession is all he's ever really learned from life.

He bends toward home now, toward the sanctuary of his small projects. Thank God for Josephine Street, he thinks. Thank God for Lucy Kreel, née Devore, and the modest port in the storm she gave him. It might not be enough for genius, but then maybe nothing is in this day and age, as old Gaspar would probably second in a heartbeat. Things are just too depthless and ephemeral. And maybe it's all anyone can do now to say this, or to hate it. Indeed, Milo feels a kind of inspiration at the thought, an urge to bring the parts of his life together into a single overriding statement, not of genius or passion, but of outrage at a modern world grown too toxic for either. This would be all the permission he needed to get started at last on the grand seascape that would give his life the shape it's never had. He can almost see its surf line now, its reefs popping up perfect peaks, the papery remains of "By the Wind Sailors" strewn along the beach after their thousand mile trips across the ocean, a seal with two pups hauled up by a rim of weathered driftwood—all of it a huge middle finger thrust at the modern world. He almost can't wait to start.

When he gets home, however, he notices the intrusive sound of a hammer coming from the construction site next door. No matter where he goes, kitchen, living room, bedroom, the sound pursues him. There's no way he can concentrate on a new painting with that racket, and isn't it always the same? Just when the mood strikes to work on what matters, some trivial detail comes along to kill his inclination and trap him in the commonplace. He imagines the carpenter next door, a big brawny guy with only one eye in his head, a lonely cyclops banging idiotically away in the half-finished depths, and wants to throttle him.

And now that he feels so paralyzed, he looks around at his own house and sees how much work it needs. Grease on the stovetop that has to be scrubbed away, dust heaped into corners crying out for a broom, crap of every useless description cluttering each surface and empty space. He sees dead clocks, a guttered out candle, a broken sand dollar hanging on a nail, a bass lure made with a cork and a black plastic mouse, locks with no keys, a fish and game rule book from 1979, a box of spackle, a tin full of marijuana seeds, a receipt for "Eight Painted Cherubs: $125 each for a total of $1000," a cigar box full of tiny glass elephants, a World War II signal gun that doesn't work, a strapless 5D red patent leather pump, on and on. He contemplates a bout of late spring cleaning but doesn't know where to begin, which normally means he won't begin at all, only yield, as he so often has before, to the slow accumulation of things.

The hammer now resounds like two marbles the size of baseballs struck together with such force it makes him jump each time. It goads him out to the backyard, where the situation is no better. Gaping knot-holes in the shed, the dead greenhouse infested with snakes, elm saplings thickening into tropical forest, the crabgrass riotously overgrown, oxalis everywhere. He feels a need for some kind of order. His pulse begins to race and his breath fluctuates. He fills the standing bowls with more water and attacks the clumps of crabgrass by the greenhouse panes. He yanks one back and starts at the sudden sound of a *clunk!* by the elms across the yard. In silence he waits to see who, or what, the offender might be. Then he yanks at the grass again. *Clunk!* Shit. It's only him: a rusted length of pipe he used once for a swing entangled in rhizomatic stems and jammed against the bole of a sapling. Action at a distance. Interconnections so extended, you never know what the causes and effects really are, or where they might appear.

At that moment he hears "Hello!" ring out from the front yard. Emerging from under the canopy of the Adonis tree comes a tall pear-shaped man with sloping shoulders and a head like an adze. His name is Bob Last, and he's the regular supplier of Milo's shake, there to deliver a new bag. Milo's heart rarely leaps on the occasion of a visit by Bob, since he's about the mopiest guy he knows. He's one of those people who's never had a break in his life, who wasn't blessed with anything, not smarts, not looks, not luck, not confidence. His saving grace is that he's basically a decent guy who doesn't hate the deck because it was stacked against him.

Milo's half-glad to see him for once. The two of them head into the living room to conduct their business in private. He turns on the radio and hears a mandolin solo in full career.

"Do you know this song?" he asks Bob, who's busy making himself comfortable on the sofa.

"No."

"Get out of my house!" cries Milo. "That's 'Orange Blossom Special'—the greatest blue grass song of all time."

"Oh yeah. I hear it now. It's in the breakdown."

"Did you know Chet Atkins taught Mark Knopfler how to play blue grass turnarounds?"

"Is that a fact?"

"I heard the two of them just the other night. Chet Atkins was playing all these hot rock-n-roll guitar licks country style, flat pickin' them." Milo reaches over to grab his mandolin from where he'd last left it perched against a speaker. He limbers up his fingers by playing along with the radio. Bob sits back and listens.

After a while Milo says, "How you doing?"

"Not so good. My mom's got cancer."

"Really? That's a shame. A crying shame. I'm sorry to hear it."

"It's in her pancreas, and it's already spread pretty far. They don't hold out much hope."

"She's such a sweet old lady."

Bob sighs. Milo feels sad, wondering what it must be like to be as hapless as his friend. He can almost see the folded, birdlike bones in Bob's shoulders, the flesh hanging from them like fluted curtains bunched up around his waist. A bag of bones. He's never been in shape as long as Milo's known him.

"I was just down at the clinic," Bob says, "and the doctor was telling me about the cancer. He says a cell is programmed to divide only a certain number of times before it dies. But sometimes this process gets fucked up. The gene that prevents tumors gets altered, or the mechanisms inside the cell break down. That's when it becomes cancerous. It goes on dividing, making thousands of copies of itself, till it becomes a tumor. And it'd go on like that forever if it could, if the host body would let it."

Milo nods, preoccupied with the complicated number by Dan Hicks that has succeeded 'Orange Blossom Special.' "It's like the cell forgets to die, you know?" Bob says. "It forgets how to die."

It's the horns that give him trouble. He can't hear the chords. Someone ought to pass a law against horn sections in Texas swing, he silently opines. But he can't keep up, so he stops trying. "It's a crying shame," he says again.

"They're all pretty nice down at the clinic," Bob goes on. "But it's gloomy there, too. Man, is it gloomy."

"Hospitals are dangerous places. I've known more than one person who went in healthy and came out dead."

He can't believe he just said that, but Bob, bless his soul, doesn't seem to mind. "The patients are all pretty sick, because it's just for people with cancer."

"I bet the doctors are first-rate," says Milo.

"Today it smelled awful."

"Yeah?"

"And there was Jack, screaming."

"Jack? What's he doing in a cancer ward?"

"He was next door, in the rehab center. I was sitting in my mom's room and heard yowling through the window. I said to myself, 'That cat sounds familiar,' so I went over to check it out and found Jack strapped down in a bed, freaking out."

"I just saw him this morning," says Milo. "He was fine."

"The nurse said his sponsor had him committed."

Jack's had quite a day. After he left panic-struck for the clinic and his ration of methadone, he tore ass in his Mercury across town, violating about a dozen laws by the time he turned onto Hornblower Street, one long block away. In his desperation to get there by eight, when the clinic closed its doors on all laggards, he let the car drift into the other lane. Fortunately, no one else happened to be driving at the time, but he did sideswipe every parked car on the block before screeching to a halt in the clinic parking lot at two minutes past the hour. He knew he was done for when the ditzy lady who's always late, even after she moved into an apartment across the street, darted out of her front door in her nightgown. Her frizzy hair flew every which way, and she was screaming, "Don't close! Don't close!" as loud as she could, right up to the point they both arrived at the locked door.

Jack didn't know what to do. He needed that methadone bad. He already couldn't think straight or even see straight because of it. He got back into his car and headed down Hornblower Street in the direction he'd come. Once again he drifted into the other lane and sideswiped every car parked on the block. At the corner he stopped by a liquor store. He went in and bought a couple of beers, which he drank while striking up a conversation with the Mexican guy behind the counter.

He came back out a half an hour later. By then people had discovered what happened to their cars. They stood around looking at the dented doors and speculating about the perpetrator. Jack, feeling amiable after the beers, wandered up to them, pointed back at his dented doors and said, "Look at that shit! Somebody hit my car, too!"

That was just the beginning of a quest to placate the bully of dope, which would end back at the rehab center hours later. Milo hears all about it when he arrives to see if Jack's all right. He finds him in an otherwise empty day room. His wrists and ankles are tied down, and he squirms in the bed, struggling to get free. His eyes are fixed in horror on a television screen, where the local news show reports on a tropical storm in St. Croix. He can't stop screaming.

"The jumbies! Holy fucking shit! The jumbies! Don't you see them?" he asks Milo, jerking his head at the television. Milo sees wind howling through streets, waves pulverizing embankments, and bent palm trees, but none of the walking dead. "On the beach, right there, swarms of them," cries Jack. "All over the place. In the trees, they're just sitting there, laughing! Help! Help!"

Milo steps over and snaps off the television. Jack, bereft, breathes noisily for a few moments. Milo asks, "Are you high, Jack?"

"Me?" he says shiftily. "No way. No fucking way. A few beers. Seven or eight cups of coffee. Cigarettes. Smoked a joint. No, two joints. The Percodans for my back. The tranquillizers. Dextroamphetamine plus Amobarbital. Oh yeah. Popped those synthetic heroin pills, too. Some codeine cough medicine. Shot of brandy. A little hash oil. One line of speed this guy turned me onto..."

And so on. It turns out Jack broke rule number one and shot the monster of heroin at about 11 o'clock this morning. The rest of the day has been spent on a frenzied rampage through time and space, through Charlotte Amalie, New York, Mexico, Panama, the world. He's been landing a seaplane at that fishbowl airport in San Juan, Puerto Rico. It feels like he's diving in a submarine when the plane hits the water and the windows fill with spray. The tide's been turning at the locks near the

Tri-Borough Bridge when he was fifteen, and the whole heaving Long Island Sound rushes into the East River underneath his father's boat. He's been sprinkling honey water on his bales in Big Sur, even though Milo doesn't approve. He's been trying to convince him that people like it. He says, "Milo, man, when I don't do it, people complain. They're always telling me, 'Jack, this stuff ain't so good, you know, it don't got that sweet taste, you hear what I'm saying...?'" Hippolyta is bitching again about the hot tub parties while these sexy half-French, half-black girls with attitude are dancing on stilts. It's Mardi Gras. Carlos Calderon is teaching a wigged out Cuban transvestite dressed like a peacock the words to "I Can't Get No (Satisfaction)" while sipping piña coladas on his Grebe motor yacht. He's been living on an abandoned tobacco plantation in the Everglades, right after Tariq took over the Empire, swimming every day in this creek. One day an old Seminole Indian comes up and says, "You swim in there?" and Jack says, "Sure, why not?" The Indian says, "Alligators, that's why not. It's full of them." He's been reliving the time the Jamaican jumbies robbed him of a shipment of needles and rolling papers for the good junkies of Charlotte Amalie. He was their patron saint at the time, and maybe he still is. The jumbies kept him tied up all night long. They swarmed in the mangrove swamps, in the lemon trees, with the toucans in the old lady's attic room at Nahual, pointing shotguns at his head and screaming inexplicably, "Soon come mon! Soon come mon!"

By late afternoon Jack had procured an Uzi machine gun from an old neighbor down in the beach flats and was standing in the middle of a street randomly spraying the tops of palm trees with bullets. He told passersby he was "tree-trimming," but he knew it was the jumbies and he was raining annihilation upon them.

Not too long after that he found himself in the clinic strapped to the bed. Nurse Ratshit was needling him mercilessly. "Cat got your tongue?" she asked. "Shhh! Go quiet as a cat. Don't let the cat out of the bag! Are you a cat without a grin, or a grin without a cat? When the cat's away, the mice will play. He-he-he."

Milo doesn't know what to say. He's admired, awed, and envied his friend like most other people who know him for his swashbuckling spirit, but he can see now the dark side of Jack's glamor in the tendons that start out from his neck as if he were an epileptic. Behind his freedom lies this strain, this compulsion, this craving for sublimity or release that only traps him in his most fallible urges. The proof is something Jack once admitted about heroin: that after the first time, it's never really the same, and before too long you take it just to feel normal. Normal, on heroin! How is it, Milo enquires, that the feeling of transcendence comes to be ordinary, god-like rush a quick path to the trivial? Are all our pirates, nomads, and rock stars only emblems of a secret passivity, a need to give ourselves over to the world in immediate and total submission?

In any case it's no way to live, stepping gingerly between the Pusher Man and the rehab center. Milo understands this when he goes over to the Crystal Palace and collects some clothes, a razor, a toothbrush, and toothpaste for Jack to use during his mandatory 48-hour incarceration. The place is covered with glass dust. There's glass dust on people's cars outside, glass dust coating the grass and bushes in the yard, slurries of glass dust on the linoleum floors leading into the ward where Jack keeps these big motorized barrels and huge piles of untumbled glass. No wonder he coughs all the time. The dust is silica—breath it in long enough and you aggravate the cilia in the lungs and get silicosis. Jack's killing himself in more ways than one. He's a smart guy, probably the smartest Milo knows. But he doesn't reflect, there's nothing reflective about him at all. Whatever happens, he never looks back.

Milo passes into the area where Jack keeps his inventories of paperweights, snowglobes, wands, etc. It's one lonely place, for all the signs of vigorous industry. Threadbare curtains blow gently in over torn plaster fallen from the roof above, and stains like grooves on the walls make Milo think of crazy people rubbing shoulders up against them. Jack's room resembles the inner sanctum of a squat house. A mattress with tangled sheets, an Indian hookah, a few New Yorker magazines on the floor, a reprinted painting from olden times of twin boys with mongoloid faces perched on white ruffs, are the only signs of human habitation. No wonder he shows up for dinner as often as he does. The place feels like a bad dream.

Back at the clinic, Jack has settled down enough to know where he is and to grasp that he's going to have to stay a while. He tries to make the best of a bad situation. "I've had some terrible luck lately, it's true," he says. "But it's turning around. I can feel it. The pendulum always swings back for me. I don't know how to explain it. Good luck runs in my family. My grandfather, he was lucky. He fought for the Austrians in the First World War. They made him charge the enemy in their trenches even though he knew it meant death for sure. It was his job to get killed. They made all the poor people, Slavs, Jews, gypsies, the shitworkers, go in first so the Italians would use up their ammunition. My grandfather wouldn't do it, so this hussar rode up on a horse and said, 'Either you charge the bastards, or I kill you where you stand.' Then he drew his sword and raised it over his head, and my grandfather had no choice but to run onto the bat-tlefield with all the other Schlemiels. Well, guess what? He charged on out there scared shitless and watched as every single soldier was killed except him. The Italians routed them. He was the only one who survived! Even that hussar got whacked."

"No kidding," says Milo drily.

"He cut loose from the army that day and later on became an optician. He made lenses for spectacles, opera glasses, pocket telescopes. I remember when I was a kid, the old guy was practically blind, just this crazy old immigrant in New York. The only thing he used to say was, '*Occe! Occe! Lov-e-ly occe!*' over and over again."

Milo may have been mistaken when he assumed that Jack had no capacities for reflection or that no reflection could be a practical possibility for anybody. He seems keen enough for it now. Milo lets him talk as the light in the room fades with the setting sun.

"If it wasn't for my grandfather, I probably never would have gotten into glass. Glass and me go way back. My aunt used to make stained glass windows. I used to play around with those leaded rods, 'came' she called them—which was always a joke, because she was pretty hot when I was a kid—and watch her make stained glass dragonflies or some shit like that. Yeah," he says, nodding, "it all fits together. Nothing's accidental really. Luck is a puzzle. All you gotta do is figure it out. I can feel it coming on already. Good days are ahead."

He continues like this a while more before starting in on one of his standard fade outs. One minute he's jabbering away, the next he's fast asleep. Milo tiptoes into the lobby and tells the nurse. Then he drives home in his old VW Squareback, letting the familiar chirp and rasp of the motor soothe his nerves. He loves that sound. It's as if a bunch of cicadas and butterflies were flying around inside there; that's how it moved the pistons. Other people have heard the same thing. They say the car belongs in a field somewhere, not on the road.

He pulls into his driveway with the dregs of dusk over East Brother. He goes out to the street to collect his mail, tired all of a sudden. As he's sifting through the usual assortment of bills and advertisements, an old lady scuttles down the middle of the street like a crab, glowering at him. It's Mrs. Farnsworthy, his neighbor at the end of the block. She lives in a ranch house with a paved yard painted the color of grass, and that's all Milo's ever needed to know about Mrs. Farnsworthy. She and her doddering husband have a flagpole and keep an RV parked on the street. Their front door opens straight into their living room, and during the day he can hear the sounds of their television played at full blast on account of deafness.

"Hey!" she calls out peremptorily. "When are you going to cut back that hedge?"

He doesn't feel like getting into an argument now. The day has started to weigh him down. "You're catching me at the wrong time, Mrs. Farnsworthy."

"When are you going to sweep up all those leaves?"

"I don't go telling you how to run your house, so you just let me run mine the way I want to."

"Can't you see it's a fire hazard?"

"There hasn't been a fire here in a hundred years."

"I'm going to call the Fire Marshall and tell him there's a fire hazard."

"Come on!"

"I'm calling the Fire Marshall first thing in the morning," she says again, clacking her claws as she passes by. "It's a disgrace."

Milo loses his temper. "Fuck you," he says to her departing back. "Fuck you! Fuuuuck youuuu!!"

His voice rings out in the cooling night air. He's not talking to Mrs. Farnsworthy anymore, but to all of East Brother. And he realizes that he hates it, deeply and bitterly, with a resentment as layered in him as the years of waiting for a world that never gave its promised embrace. He peers in both directions of the now deserted street. Yucca spikes, agave corollas, the massive head of a giant palm tree form their still geometries down the opposite sidewalk. A scent of night-blooming jasmine makes his senses reel. The moment is strangely riveting, like a magnified heartbeat. But nothing is there behind the appearances and Milo knows it. It's exactly nothing. East Brother is not real at all.

He goes inside to switch on the lights and open the gas burners on his stove for some heat. After that he rolls a cigarette. The house is still, expectant. The medallions strewn about the kitchen stare back at him saying, "I'm done! You don't have to work on me no more!" This calms him down. He can hate more steadily now, hate the old ladies, the guys from the Lion's Club, the cops, the contractors, the real estate salesmen. Maybe he should leave, take up Harry Contento's offer, repugnant as it is, and get the hell out, before the hate gets to be too much. Go live in the Northern California woods or down on the beach at San Blas. Listen for the thrash of that iguana underneath the hacienda. They've fucked everything up too much here to believe in it anymore. What's he waiting for? Leave. Leave now.

But he knows, with a part of him as steady and thorough as any hate, that he won't do it. As much as his heritage house is a burden, he loves it the way you would an old mule who's worked hard for you all its life. He shares with it the intimacy of doing a job together, and even if you and that mule don't do the job very well, you come to know each other's limitations and even rely on them. What doesn't he know about this place? The foundation is made of horizontal redwood slats laid in mud. There's horsehair mixed in the lathe and plaster walls. The windows have little teardrop-shaped bubbles in the glass. The house has settled here and shifted there. What shingles remain on the roof are so dried out the rain passes right through them, water damage has warped the sheeting boards beneath, and termites are eating away at the pink redwood rafters. Mildew has colonized the closets. Bone salt corrodes the board and batten slats outside.

Somehow, though, it all still holds together, on this side of ruin. Milo feels the sinew of his relation to the house as tough and fibrous as ever, and the organ to which it clings is his heart, dumb thing that it is. He retrieves Lucy's diary from its box in the living room and leafs through the foxed pages, rereading the entries. "January 6, 1914: The men cut hay, made their post by noon, fooled all day on the landing. Elsie's gonna kitten, James is a cairful hand with a boiler. Staid in today, tinkered and did my flannel, foagy afternoon, tem. 70 wind NW." He places his nose at the binding and breathes in the musty past. He wishes he could turn cars back into thick-wheeled phaetons, airplanes into flying balloons, ships into tall ships, and East Brother into a barren, rocky hillside with dunes.

"April 14, 1914: Feeling spry today, went to Catalina, picked wild strawberries, a right pleasant visit, Ed going on with his joaks, TD Winks very good duet."

Now what in the hell does that code mean? The mystery is killing him, but he can't figure it out and soon gives up trying. He steams a clutch of asparagus, makes a ham and cheese sandwich, and sits down at the kitchen table to eat. Outside, in the upper reaches of the elm trees, he hears the mockingbird start up its nightly carol. For how long have mockingbirds been showing up here at springtime, heading south again in autumn? he wonders. A thousand years and more. He consoles himself with the likelihood that this fractured litany sounds pretty much the way Lucy heard it back in the early days. She probably sat right where he is now and heard the same gibberish kick-started a little later each night. There is, he sees now, a perennial streak in nature that gladdens the heart in spite of everything transient and modern. Robins, traveling south for the winter, hang around his yard and wait for the first rains to draw worms up out of the ground. In October the bees disappear from the hummingbird feeder, and the fruit flies go away. Blue birds, orioles, finches with their red hoods, all take up residence here in springtime. It's regular as clockwork. Little miracles of renewal connecting him to a more fundamental world, if he'll only let them.

Right then all equanimity vanishes. Horror strikes deep into his heart. Through the window he's just seen a woman, hunched over and white as a sheet, flit by and vanish in the darkness of the backyard. Holy shit, he thinks, and immediately fishes his Bowie knife out of a drawer.

It's the Gray-Haired Lady, come to torment him in her alcoholic haze. He turns the lock in the kitchen door. As he does, he sees her again, standing just beyond the porch under the Adonis tree. She cuts the perfect figure of a witch, pale and slight, glaring back at him with bleak, angry eyes. The tangled branches behind her writhe like snakes in her vast Medusa's head. Luckily, it's not turning him to stone.

"Go away, Mariah," he yells through the door.

"I want to talk to you."

"Well, I don't want to talk to you."

"Who do you think you are?" she barks. "I'm a person, goddammit. And I'm out here in the fucking cold. You don't have the right not to talk to me."

She steps onto the porch and bangs the windowpane.

"I'm not letting you in," says Milo, staring at the rings that carve themselves into her chalky cheeks.

"I'm not leaving until you do."

"I'm calling the cops then."

"Go ahead, call them! In fact, I'll make it easy for you. Rape!!" she screams. "Raaaaape!! Raaaaape!! This fucker's raping me!!"

Milo opens the door, making sure the Bowie knife is prominent enough for her to know it's there.

She walks in, suddenly calm. "How you doing?"

"What do you want, Mariah?"

"Nothing." She darts wolfish glances around the room.

"I don't have any liquor. You should know that by now."

"I don't want a drink," she says. "What makes you think I'm drinking?"

"Well, for starters, your eyes look like a couple of tomatoes dropped in buttermilk."

"You always assume the worst, Milo. You never give me the benefit of the doubt."

The injustice of this observation deserves the silence he gives it.

"I've been sober for five months. I just stopped by to see how you were doing. Like a regular person."

"I'm not interested in hashing this out anymore," he says.

"Why not?"

"Because we've been through it a hundred times before."

"You're not a regular person," she says, nodding manically. "That's your problem. You're always depressed. You gotta get over it, Milo. Look around you. This place is a fucking dump—"

"I'm calling the cops," he bristles, and heads off to the living room.

"You gotta straighten out," she says, following behind. "It's people like you who keep people like me from wiping ourselves up off the floor." She fixes her gaze on some far away point, caught in the lie. Tears start in her eyes.

Milo has the phone at his ear and is dialing 911. But he doesn't hit the green button on the keypad.

She sits on the sofa and cries. "You don't know what it's like living on welfare checks. My landlord's kicking me out of my house, Milo. They're about to shut off my water. My kid's in jail again. His old man split and I can't pay bail this time. You hear me? I can't get my kid out of jail!"

"Hello. I'd like to report a trespasser at 1234 Josephine Street. That's right..."

"You heartless sonofabitch!" she cries. "I'm telling you I'm in pain and need help, and you rat on me to the cops."

He puts the phone down. "They're on their way."

"I'm desperate, Milo. I just need a...a little loan. A hundred bucks, that's all. I swear to God."

"No."

"I won't spend it on booze, I promise."

"Bullshit."

"I've changed," she says. "You don't know, but I've changed. It's just that nothing else in my life has changed, too."

"Aren't you on probation, Mariah?"

"Nobody gives a damn about me. Nobody ever has. You don't know what that's like—"

"What are you going to do when the cops get here?"

"All you care about is yourself," she sneers. "You know what they call somebody like you at AA? A narcissist, that's what. It's just you and your fucking navel."

Milo knows the instant he gets into it with her, the game is lost. They might yell at each other all night long, which is exactly what she wants because it's a way to get through, to force an interlocutor where otherwise she'd only have herself to berate. Milo's a straw man she talks to so as not to talk to herself.

"How come you spend so much time alone, huh?" she asks. "That's not normal. It means you're not open to experience. You live in fantasy worlds and deny reality."

"You sound like a social worker."

She ignores this. "Well, I'm not a fantasy, you hear me? I'm a real woman, with real flesh and blood needs."

"It's not my problem—"

"*I'm not a ghost!*" she screams, sounding as if she's not quite sure whom she needs to convince.

"You're not my old lady either!" He can't help himself.

"You wouldn't know what to do with a real woman if you found one," she scoffs. "She'd ask you to be a real man, and sometimes I wonder about you, Milo. I really do."

"This is thin ice you're walking on..."

"I wonder if you've got the right kind of drive, you know what I mean?"

"Thin fucking ice."

"Are you queer?"

Milo snaps. "Get out of my house." He grabs her by the shoulders and drags her kicking and screaming to the front door. "You fucking weaselly-assed bitch." He opens it, pushes her outside, and slams it shut behind her, turning the lock. A furious tirade ensues. She walks around to the back yard as he takes refuge in the kitchen, maligning his manhood for all the neighborhood to hear. He has no choice but to wait her out, outlast the spending of her venom, and hope she gets desperate and lonely enough to leave. He turns up the radio as loud as he can stand it and heads for his drafting table. He clears away a space and lays down a sheet of paper. He takes out his collection of watercolor pans and squeezed tubes, draws close a coffee can with water in it, and readies his brushes. Then he stares at the white sheet and draws a total blank.

He doesn't hear Mariah anymore. He turns the radio down again and cracks open the front door to see if she's still there. Nothing. He walks around the house to the side porch and squints into the dark yard. The only sound is the mockingbird yapping away in the high trees. He goes out to the street to find her Volvo gone. The coast is clear.

He returns to his table and sets to work mixing watercolors, hoping that will lift his spirits some. The whisper of an idea passes through his consciousness, but it never gains in tone enough for him to hear it. Something is missing, a sense...of the whole, that's what: of fragments swirled together like blackbirds flocking. They almost want to, pulled forward by that mysterious ability to swerve in unison, but they shy away again, lose the pattern, collapse in cross-purposes.

He dips a sponge in water, wets the sheet of paper, and applies a graded wash of cerulean blue with a flat brush. He tilts the table slightly so the paint can spread and flow. He lifts out some color here, drips wet pools of color there, and begins to compose a long breaking wave. He paints in a cadmium red sky dissolving from subtle granulations to a vivid band of translucent scarlet, where the sun has but lately escaped this earth. After that he adds the burnt umber cone of a sea stack. When the first wash has dried a little, he scrapes the surface with sandpaper to create mottled white highlights in the frothy parts of the wave. He works the scene through successive layers and it gains in moody expressiveness. Milo knows how to paint waves—ankle-biters on a still summer day or bone-crushing fifteen-foot swells with an offshore wind going. It doesn't matter. He's got about fifty of them in a pile right beside him. But the wave of all waves, the one breaking in his soul too deep for capture in light, once more eludes him. It probably always will. He's well beyond the time that comes when failure has to be accepted as a destiny, or rather a man's separation from his destiny has to be regarded as permanent, stained into the fibers of his existence. At some point there's no getting around it.

Bored now, he goes into the kitchen and tunes his portable TV to the local news. "Reports have been confirmed today that a clinic specializing in human cloning has been in operation since early last year," relates an earnest young Asian woman. The scene cuts to a long shot of a nondescript medical building. "Here in this Mexico City laboratory, Dr. Leonard Fishbein, long a pioneer in the cloning of headless human bodies for the purpose of organ donation, has announced the birth of Sam Lacks, a clone of Jerome Lacks of Phoenix, Arizona. Lacks, a—"

Milo can't believe it. We're cloning humans, and she sounds as if it's just another case of insurance fraud or a janitor strike. He turns the channel to a repeat of

*Seinfeld.* George is twisting his face in squeamish dread at the punchline of a joke. He says, "—a laxative on account of my cooonstipaaaashun!"

Hmm. Milo turns the channel to a commercial. "Relax again at our luxurious seaside resort..."

Once more he turns it, this time to a sitcom about middle-class black kids and their problems. "—you'll axe a stupid question, and git a stupid answer..." Laugh track.

He turns it to a British stage production of *Two Gentlemen of Verona.* A man in a gold chasuble moans: "Alack sad yeoman!"

Fuck. How in the hell is that possible? And why isn't someone here to witness it, to prove Milo isn't crazy? There never are with coincidences like these. They don't exist even when they do.

A general dullness of spirit, growing on him for some time now, announces itself as the revenant throb of his infected tooth. He takes a couple aspirin and smokes a cigarette, holding the smoke in his lungs for as long as he can. This settles him down. His mind is a swirl of different thoughts. He needs to fix his attention on one thing. The television, he realizes, is vying senselessly with the radio in the other room. He turns it off and takes the book he's reading, a sea adventure called *Forty Fathom Deep,* to his bedroom upstairs. He reads for a while laid out on his bed, but he can't focus or forget the pain. His consciousness is dispersed like noise, dulled yet acutely audible. It occurs to him that a torturer might be struck by the possibilities in making dullness acute like this. Never to be able to tune out the static of one's own mind would be cruelty indeed.

Goddam that mockingbird! He's the interfering signal in Milo's sound field right now, outside delivering his demented symphonies to the hushed night air. He can be a royal pain in the ass, especially in moments like this one, compounded of ache and tedium. He throws his book down and holds his hands over his ears, but he can't keep himself from listening. Are those the sharp staccato notes of a banjo? How did it learn to choke a guitar string like that? Wait a minute. Is that the melody of "Coal Black Chicken" he hears in between the firing of that piston? He was just running that through his head a minute ago. Shit. The eel of paranoia juts out from its crevice in Milo's rip-rap. It seems as if a correspondence way too neat between his brain and that mockingbird betrays a design beyond the abilities of chance and nature to improvise. He hovers on the edge of a suspicion. Maybe it's not a real mockingbird out there. Maybe an enemy of his, someone who knows him well, who knows how to get under his skin, is out there in the elm saplings with a reed pipe, mimicking a mockingbird.

The intuition of another trespasser possesses Milo to take a flashlight into the yard and check it out. He tiptoes to the apple-pear tree and stands quietly in the dark. The scent of night-blooming jasmine is rank. He can see the moon in the trees. A breeze is shaking tiny yellow flowers from the Adonis tree and stirring dry leaves off the roof. He looks into the lit kitchen through the window and thinks how cozy it seems from the outside. He surprises himself in the odd conceit of a stranger wondering about the person whose home this is, whether he's sad or happy, fulfilled or frustrated. For a minute he has no idea. Whoever it is, he hopes the guy's smart enough to see what a good thing he has.

He has a good thing. It's a magical place. He thrills to the thought that he could be anywhere now, in any time or in no time at all, in that perennial present where everything stands out, perfect and still. He thinks, *This is beautiful. What more could you want? What could be missing in something so complete?* But something is missing. He can tell by how lonely it makes him feel to say it, how cut off in the knowledge that this beauty is complete because it does without him altogether, does without everything and refers only to itself. Life surrounds him root and branch, in tendrils of smilax and the snares that spiders weave. It turns in cycles of an awesome fecundity. But he senses its remoteness, too, like a humming you hear only as the susurration of blood in veins. Home has this schizoid dimension for Milo, this quality of uncommunicable experience and dizzy solipsism.

It really is a mockingbird up there. He ceases his song when Milo beams his flashlight into the branches. They're feeling each other out. Who are you? *Who are you?* I live here. *So do I.* I'd like to get some sleep tonight. *I'm just doing my thing.* Aren't we all? *Amen, brother.*

A knock, coming from the vicinity of the shed, draws Milo to the rickety door, which he practically pulls off its hinges on opening. It smells like the streets of Laredo inside: bygone and wild. A ray of moonlight slants crisply between two ceiling slats, raking past dense curtains of cobweb and dust. He sweeps his flashlight over the shelves that line one wall and down to a dead oscilloscope that used to belong to his dad. He enters, rummaging in emptiness. Yes, indeed, not a lot to hold on to here: an old longboard, a wicker basket full of seashells, a macramé owl, and a heat gun for shrink rap—more refuse and lumber of his disordered life. Milo has the feeling that he's not really here in the shed, that this is one interlude of a long day lived in a dream. The real question is, who's dream is he? And what life will he vanish into on waking?

Needing a touchstone to ground him again, he gets it when he comes to a lugbox and finds a big fat mama possum with her white kitteny kids—the source of the knock. They lift their blind eyes into the beam of light and scowl mutely up at him. Here's a surprise! He always liked possums. People think of them as big rats, but they're smarter and cuter, too. Their claws are more like fingers with thick pads on them, and they have what are almost stubby thumbs that allow them to grasp things like a real hand. As he backs out of the shed, leaving them to their slumbers, and returns to the house, he remembers the time he saw six possums hanging by their tails from an apricot tree. He was ten years old and passing through an orchard in the Santa Ana Canyon, on his way to school. They picked the apricots and ate them upside down, chittering to themselves like snipey kids and having the time of their lives. He wished he could've joined them.

Once inside he takes a piss in the bathroom. The muffled sound of water tinkling in the bowl worries him. The toothache has started to affect his hearing, the high side. He should see a dentist, but he can't pay for root canals. There's just not enough money in the secret drawer, even after he gets the last installment for the medallions. He flushes the toilet and watches dirt cloud the water in the bowl. That means the pipes have leaks in them and will have to be replaced one of these days. He'll have to tear up the floorboards and dig trenches out to the sewer line. Oh boy. His back hurts just thinking about the work that'll take. It's a bad moon out there, he decides. A bad moon rising. Things aren't working too well in a lot of ways.

He breaks open Bob's new stash and gets high to ease the pain and feel less overwhelmed by it all. He sinks down into the sofa in the living room and thinks fondly back to the days he spent growing up in the Santa Ana Canyon, the greasewood hills, the dusty roads, coyotes, stiles, hip-roofed barns hung to the rafters with leather saddles that nobody used anymore, starlings clattering like a bunch of steel traps in the trees. He remembers a pet he had, Old Joe Crow. He found him when he was only a few weeks old and raised him up. Old Joe went with him everywhere. He used to ride on the handlebars of his bike with him to school. Milo'd let him free for the day, and when he came back he'd be out there, waiting for him. He'd go hiking with him in the woods and canoeing with him in the inland bays behind Newport. He tagged along on those electric afternoons at Knott's Berry Farm, waiting outside the rides or flying around while Milo shot it out with his friends in the ghost town. Old Joe got used to his freedom after a couple of years. He'd come visit only when he felt like it, landing right in the middle of a touch football game or lighting on the sill of his bedroom window with a stolen key in his beak. He kept the faith to the end of his life, better than most people Milo's known, and he always respected him for it.

Those were the days of faith and slow time, flickering like cowboy and Indian movies in the dark theatre of his memory. Actually, it's a Fox theatre with plush comfortable seats and thick velvet ropes and sticky floors. He can still smell the stale popcorn. They don't make movie theaters like that anymore. They're all gone now, like so many other things Milo knows about, that ghost town at Knott's Berry Farm, for instance, or the salt factory back up Newport Bay, or Clifton's Cafeterias, or '57 Chevys. He knows the engine of a '57 Chevy inside and out, and now it isn't good for anything. The world's gone by and trapped Milo in useless knowledge. That's the story of his life, useless knowledge. It runs like a leitmotif through the years of teenage rebellion, the early homesteading in East Brother, the struggles over how to get money, and the more recent bouts with middle-aged angst. He feels like an obsolescent engine left behind in a field, its parts fused together with rust. Maybe there's a few vines of wild morning glory twined around it, too.

In the background he recognizes the electric guitar licks coming from the radio as the handiwork of Bob Dylan. It's not one of the classic tunes, conjuring the Fifteenth Dream, Davey Moore, or Johnny in the basement mixin' up the medicine. But the song still chimes perfectly with his nostalgic mood now, reciting in a litany all the things that are broken in this modern world: threads, springs, beds, plates, gates, bottles, laws, bones, and heads, among other choice examples.

Milo's always had faith in Dylan. Total faith. He knows how to tell it like it is, straight from a broken heart. Milo could always find that point in his music where the heartache goes away or you work through it to the other side, and it's not painful anymore. That's what he's looking for. Folk singers and rock singers know how to get to that point, jamming on their guitars, bending those blue notes. They turn pain into a cry and a meaning. Milo feels the change now. Dylan's raspy voice thrums through his prone body and speaks as if to his most secret self. For he, too, knows when things break. He knows how much weight a board will take before it snaps. He knows how much to twist copper before it strips. He knows how many pounds of pressure a cylinder can handle before it blows out. He has that experience, that know-how. Maybe it's all he has.

The sofa feels warm and snug, the space around him dense as cotton-wool. With a strange lucidity he flashes on himself seated by other kids in the bed of a pickup as it rumbles through an orange grove. The sky is the color of sheetmetal. The hot sun bakes. They're tired and hungry, and all they have to eat is a bunch of oranges they've just picked as part of their summer job. Milo's eaten so many the acid burns his lips. Each bite feels like wasps stinging his mouth. He stays inside that memory for a long time, licking his flayed and blistered lips, inhabiting the silent consciousness of a ten-year-old. And that kid is thinking, with words he would not know for years and years to come, *everything is broken, everything is broken.* The truck creaks and bumps down the dusty road, hunger makes him eat more oranges, the wasps at his mouth grow still more frenzied.

After that, suddenly, he's a teenager outside the Rendezvous Ballroom in Newport Beach on a foggy night, and he's kissing his girlfriend Judy for the first time in the backseat of her mom's car. They're all elbows and knees. They feel so clumsy about sex. It left him even then contrasting that experience to his first sexual explorations when he was six, with a little girl visiting from Des Moines, Iowa. They'd been left alone on a bed while their parents caroused in the other room, and before he knew it they were petting and groping each other with an ease he would never feel again, except in fleeting moments. She was the perfect conspirator, a little person who didn't need to be handled with kid gloves, who wasn't going to flinch or take offense just because you didn't think about what you were doing all the time. Between desire and its acts there lived only their two heartbeats and a marvelous contingency. No matter how easy and pleasurable love might get with Judy later on, or with any other girlfriend for that matter, it never quite rated with the innocence Milo felt with someone he would never see again and can't even picture in his head anymore. He can't even remember her name. But, in a sense, she's been the polestar for all his later longings, guiding him to certain people rather than others, to the cottage and East Brother, toward the preservation of play and reverie in this world despite all the odds. It's funny how a perfect stranger can have so much influence on the course of a life.

From the phosphene night behind Milo's eyes, and as if in answer to this disquieting insight, comes a vision of Lucy walking with her stepladder along the vanished boardwalk at Calle del Oso. She sets it down underneath a carbide lamp and lifts herself up to turn the knob and extinguish the light. She's rehashing her life, too, the hard times in Normal, the courtship days with Edwin, raising her kids as a widow, her reputation among the locals as an eccentric spinster. Milo wonders if she loved her husband so much she never thought of remarrying, or, what he considers more likely, if she never really loved him and soured on people so much she preferred her own company in the sea air at night, wild and thrilling beyond every attempt to domesticate it. Ed was probably like every Kreel he's known, regular enough people without a dreaming bone in their bodies. It's not even their fault. They've got corners on the tops of their heads. He can't imagine Ed the hardware store owner ever romancing Lucy, but...wait...at that instant it dawns on him what "TD winks" means. Solo, duet, chorus. Lucy's—and Ed's...Ed without Lucy, Ed and Lucy both, Ed and Lucy at the same time. Holy shit! Milo bursts out laughing. Ed must not have been such a sad sack after all. He assumed Victorian prudery from what Lucy said in the diary proper—stuff about pecks on the cheek under the mistletoe before church and holding hands on his folks' porch swing, tame shit like that. Meanwhile, he's fucking her out behind the water closet. Milo will be damned.

In more ways than one. Pleasure collapses too quickly into a queasy misgiving. He's not sure he wanted to know about Lucy's orgasms. He might be too close to the intimate life of a ghost, and if he's not mistaken, there are rules against that. As so often happens in these nostalgic fevers that come over him, things eventually reach a point of saturation and begin canceling themselves out. Lucidity of mind becomes a delirium into which pour all the shadowy doubts that have attended him through life like a gaggle of fallen angels. In fact he knows very little about Lucy, despite all his efforts to make her a familiar. Behind them is a strangeness he's never been able to dispel, even when it seems she's right there with him, pottering through the rooms, picking mites out of the flour jar, trimming rose bushes in the yard. For the past is gone now, and like the field after townhouses are built there, it might as well never have existed. He remembers the destruction of that natural world he grew up in: Joe Miller the rancher selling off his orange grove to build a freeway on-ramp; the rapid encroachment of subdivisions, superblocks, and cul-de-sacs on burro bush, prickly pear, and rattlesnake habitat; and the appearance, one day, of a piss yellow line in the sky, where huge chains of molecular fluorocarbons bumped up against the inversion layer. Even then, Milo knew that line passed through a lot more than air and smog. It passed through the horsehair snares and eggplant patches of his soul. It plunged arrow-like into the bull's eye of his broken heart.

He slumps ever deeper into his sofa, watching the past swirl through his mind. He siphons gas full of dirt from a tractor to put into his pickup, and an angry farmer comes up behind and thwacks him on the back of the head. He presses his finger into sunburned skin on his shoulder while floating on an inner tube down the Santa Ana River, and the white patch evanesces like a sunspot.

When he turns a winch over an irrigation well, an owl takes fright. He watches a bright red starfish annihilate a population of limpets and hermit crabs in a tide pool by Reef Point. He surprises his Swedish girlfriend Malin on her birthday by drawing her name in gasoline on the beach and lighting it so she could see it from the Ferris wheel on the boardwalk. These memories draw up the cold bottom waters of his affection till it feels as if he's drowning. Where is he? Wait a minute. It's night in Joe Miller's orange grove. He's riding his bike blindly between two rows of trees, blindly through the ether of his childhood, running into spider webs as thick as chain link fences. He stops to shake out a sun spider from his shirt. When he looks up, he sees the phosphorescent gleam of a shy glow-worm in the still center of the grove. He smells smoke and wonders where it's coming from. Presto-change-o! He's older, standing with his dad in what remains of that same grove while a huge pyre of burning orange trees blots out the stars. Flame licks at lopsided trunks, air pockets burst, the waxy leaves writhe and are consumed. Curiously, Milo enjoys himself. The heat warms his goosebumps away. The smoke brings tears to his eyes. The fascination of exploding and disintegrating things roots him to the spot. It grieves him to feel this voluptuous pull in toward destruction, when he understands perfectly well what will never be the same because of it. He's burning himself up in that fire, and he doesn't want to, but he does want to at the same time, with a heedlessness too much like passion not to be acknowledged and accorded some respect.

Shame rushes in on him here, and he wonders if he isn't turning into a rheumy-eyed old man lost in inanity. The house feels suddenly alien, and he's trapped in its husk of rooms, yearning for far-feint lands. There's not enough distance, he realizes. Things are too close. The spaces between them have shrunk to nothing. He remembers that, as he watched the glow-worm in the grove, he gripped the metal handlebar of his bike and could not for the life of him tell whether it was hot or cold. In that interval before he figured out which it was, a pure uncertainty opened itself up to him like the maw of a dragon. Now he watches it incinerate the grove. Such terrible splendor. The gasoline gleam on its jewel-encrusted hide prophesies the coming of the freeway. Where its tail curves and beats the ground will be the prestressed, post-tension reinforced concrete of the onramp. He feels sick all of a sudden. Nausea at everything, at himself, expands in his throat. His mouth is full of ashes and smoke, suffocating him. How textured time can be! he thinks. How like death in the moment of its arrival. There seems to be another voice crying out, crying out. What is it trying to tell him, so far away and so plaintive? "Fire! Fire! Fire!" It sounds like Jess. His nephew. A tiny voice, not used to projection. It never knew anything but the freeway onramp. It lacks even the compensations of memory. Poor Jess, lost on a sea of troubles. About time he came back. He was wondering where he'd gotten to.

Someone is shaking him. For a split second he feels bad because the flames in his head have caught in the curtains of his living room and scorched the stenciled in squares on the yellow walls. But that's silly. It's only a dream. He feels so static in that sensuous siren's song of sleep, fixed as in a tableau, and only a calling way back down the vista of his mind tells him that the backcloth is fake and the proscenium is crashing down. Hands, meanwhile, are grabbing his shoulders and pulling him away from the sofa. "The house is on fire!" Jess yells. Of course it is, thinks Milo. He staggers to his feet. Jess drags him through the hallway into the kitchen, hot as an oven and thick with smoke. His bewildered ears roar. He kicks one of the medallions as he stumbles by and thinks, *I didn't want your stupid job anyway!* The Adonis tree is a wall of violent flame blocking their way at the porch, and Milo doesn't understand why he can't bring himself to care. Jess, desperate and alert like a man on a battlefield, takes off his peacoat and wraps it around them both. Then, with a courage that will later stir Milo to tears, he grips his uncle tightly around the shoulders and leaps with him through the wallowing flames out to the driveway beyond. They fall crashing against the dirt. Milo smells burning flesh and hair. His! Jess whacks him repeatedly with the palms of his hands, stamping out a fire in his flannel shirt. "Come on!" he cries. But Milo hesitates, squinting back into the inferno. The only thing he sees is the statue of St. Francis of Assisi with the hands broken off, miraculously spared by the bed of soft moss. He runs up to the very edge of the blaze and snatches it away.

Fire trucks with their urgent, baleful sirens are converging on Josephine Street. Firemen leap out trailing their hoses behind, and two of them alertly set about rescuing the VW Squareback. Neighbors in pajamas and robes hold their hands at their mouths and gape. Jess and Milo, blackened with soot and shaggy as two hobos, stand out in the street and watch as the cypress hedge burns in a frenzy and a night breeze fans the flames into the upper reaches of the elm trees. Jess explains how he was coming home and saw smoke billowing across Josephine Street. When he ran into the sideyard, he almost bowled into a paunchy man he'd never seen before, busy pouring gasoline onto the flames. The man, frightened, dropped his can and took off, while Jess went into the house to find him asphyxiating on the couch. Milo doesn't listen. His life is going up in smoke. *His life is going up in smoke!* He can't believe it, can't wrench himself free from a webby feeling of weird nonchalance and even relief. The house is raging, as if it knew his betrayal. The roof burns off like thatch and the rafters collapse one by one into the bedrooms below. Fire eats into the enclosed eave. The firemen concentrate their efforts on either side so as to keep the conflagration from spreading to neighboring homes. This proves impossible, however, as the Adonis tree more or less abuts the half-finished summer house, and it, too, begins to burn. The blaze will last the rest of the night, forming a massive beacon visible as far away as Catalina Island.

By first light the firemen have extinguished the last embers, cordoned off the site, and left exhausted for their station. Except for a few charred studs, the cottage has melted into slurries and rivulets of ash. Only the stove is still standing in its rightful place. The blackened refrigerator lies canted on its side. The claw-footed bathtub has fallen into an oily ooze where the water pipes burst. The apple-pear tree is nothing but a stump, and skeletal elm saplings surround like groping corpse's fingers thrust up from graveyard earth.

The neighbors have all gone back inside to get some rest, grateful that today is Sunday. Only Milo and Jess remain behind. They cross the cordon and wander through the ruins, finding little relics after all: a hat-pin, a marble, the iron head of a hammer, the calipers from the kitchen table. The sky shimmers like mother-of-pearl above their heads, promising another perfect day. It's as if nothing has changed. Milo, still hugging St. Francis of Assisi, turns a knob on the stove and, applying his lighter, discovers that it still works. Jess comes up beside him and watches his uncle absorbed in contemplation of the blue flame. A silent moment passes between them.

"What are you going to do?" Jess asks at last, as delicately as he can.

Milo clears his throat. The question runs into his shocked consciousness like a gravity wave. Find another place to live in East Brother, he supposes. Get as far away as he can. Move to the Northern California woods. Stay. Watch those dolphins from the hacienda in San Blas. Go looking for pelican skulls on the beach. Go. *Go.* Never look back. Be free.

"Fuck if I know," he says with a sigh.

About the Author

STEFAN MATTESSICH has written three other novels: *Point Guard*, a coming-of-age story set on the Northern California coast of Mendocino; *The Riverbed*, about intelligent young people coming to learn about the darker sides of the suburban dream they call home; and *A Precarious Man*, about the search for love and belonging in neoliberal times. He went to Yale College and has a PhD in literature from the University of California, Santa Cruz, where he wrote a monograph on the fiction of Thomas Pynchon entitled *Lines of Flight*, published by Duke University Press. He teaches English at Santa Monica College and lives in Los Angeles.